Mrs. Alexander

The Heritage of Langdale

Vol. II

Mrs. Alexander

The Heritage of Langdale
Vol. II

ISBN/EAN: 9783337053550

Printed in Europe, USA, Canada, Australia, Japan

Cover: Foto ©Andreas Hilbeck / pixelio.de

More available books at **www.hansebooks.com**

THE

HERITAGE OF LANGDALE.

A Novel.

BY

MRS. ALEXANDER,

AUTHOR OF "THE WOOING O'T," "WHICH SHALL IT BE?" "RALPH
WILTON'S WEIRD," ETC.

IN THREE VOLUMES.

VOL. III.

LONDON:

RICHARD BENTLEY AND SON,

Publishers in Ordinary to Her Majesty the Queen.

1877.

THE HERITAGE OF LANGDALE.

CHAPTER I.

VENING was closing in on the day after the events last recorded. John Langley had returned from his daily avocations, and finished his frugal dinner he had eaten alone. Harold, never very fond of his father's society, had taken advantage of his character of an invalid to have his irregular but tolerably frequent meals and potations served upstairs. It had been a most trying period to him, this incarceration in his father's gloomy, respectable abode. But Langley was resolute ; he

knew what the consequences would be if he
left him free and unwatched in his bachelor
lodgings, so Harold was obliged to submit to
his fate, which was always his destiny whenever his father chose seriously to oppose him.
How heartily he cursed his hard fate, the
crotchets of his sire, the obstinacy and bad
taste of his intended bride, the meddling of
the insolent stranger, for it was of course
now well known who had rescued Maud—all
can be imagined, but even this mental
exercise was but poor pastime, and to show
himself with a broken arm was too dangerous
an experiment.   He therefore bore his imprisonment as best he might, to the diminution
of Mr. Langley's stock of Hollands and
Burgundy.

With his accustomed methodical habit,
John Langley turned to his accounts after
dinner, and having made sundry entries and
calculations, put away his books and ascended
to his son's room.   He found the interesting
invalid looking very pallid, dishevelled, and
unkempt.   Harold was one of those who,
wanting in innate self-respect, only care to

dress for company. He was seated by the fire, a table with a bottle and glass upon it beside him, and a dice-box in his hand.

"Good-evening to you," said Mr. Langley, drawing a chair opposite his son, and laying a letter he held on the table. "What are you doing, Harold?"

"Just throwing a main, sir, right hand against left, though the right has to trust his adversary with the bones."

"Um! I like not the pastime! How is your arm, boy?"

"So-so — a little stronger, I think; I hunger for the time when it will be able to pay my debts to that meddling foreign adventurer."

"He stands well with the Countess of Helmsford."

"Ay, sir, she is mad about him; I should not wonder if she forgot herself so far as to take him for a husband, as well as a lover."

"If that be so he is no rival of *yours?*"

"Of mine! No; it's not like he would turn from a wealthy full-blown beauty to a little beggarly white-faced chit——"

"Stay, Harold; I find people begin to speak of her as the possible heiress of Langdale! Lady Helmsford does not hesitate to say so; Craggs spoke to me only to-day to the same effect——"

"Ha!" interrupted Harold, "that's serious! Was there ever such infernal ill-luck as my being trapped at Langdale? Still, this Monteiro acted in the matter of the rescue as the devoted servant of Lady Helmsford; that is his line."

"Perhaps so, and so far 'tis better! You know I applied formally to that insolent woman for the restoration of my ward; here is her reply, most artfully worded: 'Dear Sir,'—mark that! It is little more than ten days since, with scorn, she drove me from her house, ordering her lacqueys, in my hearing, never to admit me again. Now I am 'Dear Sir,—I have your letter of yesterday's date. I do not pretend to oppose your just claim to the custody of your ward; she should be ready to accompany you to-morrow, so far as I am concerned, but she is in truth seriously indisposed and ill at ease. The physicians whom

I have called in to see her can testify to the truth of this statement—she is unable to leave her chamber. In a few days she will doubtless be better able to bear the transit, and I shall be happy to restore her to your care. Indeed, I think of returning for a season to Paris, in which case I should of course be guided by your will in the disposal of Mistress Langley.

" ' I have the honour to be, sir,

" ' Yours faithfully,

" ' E. HELMSFORD.' "

John Langley read every word of this letter down to the signature in a dry bitter tone, and then stopping, looked at his son.

" Well, sir," said the young man, reaching over to the wine and filling his glass, " it is very fair and civil. Women like coddling each other when they are sick ; we will have her here next week, and quite time enough, in my opinion."

" Do not drink more," returned Langley, pushing the bottle away ; " it seems to me you have already had too much. So—the

letter pleases you! it does not me. The
Helmsford woman did not compose that
herself; it must have cost her scornful heart
somewhat even to pen the lines; there's some
shrewd adviser pulling the wires. Moreover,
it is an object to gain a few days, and she
has gained them. I would destroy my own
character as a kind and fatherly protector,
were I to drag a sick girl from the care of
her own aunt."

"Ay, sir, but the girl may be ill; you see
she offers the witness of the physicians."

"Bah!" returned Langley with a scoff, "worth
so much per word! No, Harold, I will
fight her with her own weapons; I will
courteously assent to the delay and request
permission for my *own* doctor, in whom I
have great confidence, to visit her; trust me,
he shall soon declare her fit to travel!"

"Zounds, sir!" cried Harold, laughing, "I'll
back you against my lady; I suppose you have
a trusty medical attendant?"

"Two or three, my son—two or three,"
returned John Langley meditatively. "Next
week at furthest she must be in our hands.

I will speak her fair, assure her I will not press the marriage upon her, then you must do the rest."

"What part have you chalked out for me then ?"

"The desperate disappointed lover ; and this time there shall be no failure !"

"So it was to be last time."

"I have a better plan now. Moreover, though I care not to appear, I shall see to the execution of it myself. Listen, Harold ! as soon as I have my ward safe I will soothe her ; she shall be advised to try change for the recovery of her shattered nerves, and I will offer her a tranquil retreat at Langdale ; pledge my honour that you shall not go there, but refuse to promise that you may not molest her here ; she shall start *without* me, mind, under the care of Mathews and the doctor and some woman. I will never let that vile witch Dorothy inside my house again ! Then on the road (not too far), you, urged by despair, finding your own father against you, attack the party and carry the prize to the place before prepared ; there we can provide a priest as well as a doctor, let the ceremony be performed, after which you can be guided by your own judgment; keep her a close prisoner for a week—ten days—more—till I —getting alarmed at not having news of her safe arrival at Langdale, also at the disappearance of my son—make search and find both! By that time the haughty Mistress Maud will not refuse to acknowledge you as her husband. Her reputation will be at your mercy, and all the chances are in your favour ; besides which, away in that lonely place there are numerous means at your disposal——"

"Why, 'tis a far finer plot than t'other!" interrupted Harold; "only I wish you would give me the wine or some Hollands ; they steady a fellow's nerves, and keeping indoors makes me vapourish. Zounds! I wish my cranky cousin would give us less trouble! only just fancy, if those pirates at Langdale had not nabbed me we'd have been a steady loving couple of three or four months' date !" and Harold shivered a little.

"Your courage does not fail you, boy?" asked Langley harshly. "Remember, I recommend no violence beyond anything your own impulse might suggest; but once she is your wife, I am certain all difficulty respecting a reversal of the attainder would vanish. You would be illustrious as a daring gallant! and think of the wealth, the position, the rank, for with my interest I think I could get it extended to yourself! Come, Harold, 'tis a fair prospect worth a few hours' discomfort and a bold struggle!"

"No doubt, sir! I should be a poltroon to shrink from it!"

"Now I think 'twould be well to employ Morley in organising the attempt," resumed Langley; "he is the safest, he does not know *me*, and I have his neck in a noose; he is stowed away safely now, but the ardour of the hunt for him is a little lulled. What an ill chance it was, his pitching on that treacherous dog—that man D'Arcy!"

"Yes," said Harold, grinding his teeth; "I should like to pay him back. And the place itself," he continued, "I suppose 'tis still in a state of preparation?"

"I'll see to it. Morley shall manage that,

but he must keep out of sight. My Lord
Chedworth's people have been to Lambs' and
Hatton Garden, and all his haunts, seeking
him.   That ruffian D'Arcy told all he knew—
'twas well he knew so little."

After some more discussion of detail, John
Langley bade his son good-night, promising
that he should go forth in a coach, with
strictest privacy, next day, and, after driving
to some distant point, alight and walk a while,
determining in his own mind that this expe-
dition should be undertaken only under the
guidance and guardianship of the trusty
Mathews.

So descending to his study, John Langley
penned a brief but reasonable and courteous
reply to Lady Helmsford, made a few memo-
randa which none could understand save himself, and then retired calmly to rest, all
preliminaries for his diabolical scheme having
been settled in his own mind, and slept the
sleep of the just.

Meanwhile the innocent object of these pro-
jects against her life's happiness, Maud Langley, gladly agreed with Lady Helmsford in

the necessity for keeping her room. A couple of fashionable doctors visited her, felt her pulse, inspected her tongue, and declared Lady Helmsford's suspicion that her niece was on the verge of a brain fever was singularly correct, ordered extreme quiet, nourishing diet, and sundry large bottles of physic, which Dorothy, with many grimaces expressive of disgust and contempt, emptied into the nearest sink.

But Maud's nervous system was greatly agitated. The impending avowal promised by Monteiro to Lady Helmsford was as a sword suspended over her head. She dreaded it unspeakably, yet could not rest till it was accomplished. Moreover, whenever Monteiro's words and looks and tones recurred to her, which was very often indeed, her heart beat too fast for comfort ; but insensibly she turned to him as the one true friend she possessed— the only one of all those she now knew who was connected with her dear dead father. If she could only feel certain that he had not trifled with her aunt ! When she heard his voice she believed him utterly, but when alone doubts would spring up. And Dorothy, too, was a source of tender disturbance. She longed so much to lay her head against that good soul's shoulder, and tell her all. It seemed such disloyalty to their friendship to conceal anything—and such a thing! This sort of self-accusation gave peculiar tenderness to her manner and quite frightened her attached attendant.

"Don't tell me it is just a bit of nervousness and upset," she said to Mistress Sparrow; "the darlint is downright ill. She always was a sweet lamb; but, holy Mary! — I mean, the dear knows—she is like a crature too good to live jist now! It's all that John Langley. Ah, I wish I had my wicked will of you for one week, Langley! You wouldn't do much mischief at the end of it."

If the truth were known, the Countess of Helmsford was quite as much in need of calmants as her niece. Two whole days had passed, and save for an hour in a comparative crowd at Mistress Ferrars' supper-party, she had not seen Monteiro. He had only called once, and then she was out. The strain was more than she could endure—more, at any rate, than she would. She was a brave woman, nor quite inexperienced in wearing a mask and venturing herself in a hired chair.

Her chariot was therefore ordered at a somewhat early hour one morning ; and, after depositing her at her dressmaker's, it was dismissed. Her ladyship expected Mistress Ferrars would meet her there, and she would probably return to dine with that lady.

A little later Monteiro, who had not yet gone out, was looking over some letters which he had written, to have in readiness for the frequent opportunities to be met with at "Lambs'" for sending letters abroad, when Victor entered, with a mysterious air and a suppressed smile, to inform his master that a lady was waiting without to see him.

"A lady !" exclaimed Monteiro, a sudden hope thrilling his veins. "What lady ? not the lady we rescued ?"

"No, *pardieu !* A lady twice her size."

"Show her in," said Monteiro, with some reluctance.

In another moment the door again opened

to admit a tall woman wrapped in a long
cloak, a hood on her head, and a mask on her
face. She stood quite still till the door was
closed behind her, and then removing the
mask, showed Monteiro, as he expected, the
features of Lady Helmsford.

"What pleasant freak has brought you
here, *ma belle?*" cried Monteiro kindly and
frankly, as he took her hand and led her to a
seat; "no new troubles, I hope! Take off
your cumbrous cloak and tell me everything.
No fresh attempt on the part of John
Langley?"

"No," returned Lady Helmsford, who
seemed strangely confused for so self-pos-
sessed a lady. "No; he will, I think, keep
quiet for a while. It was to speak about
yourself, Juan, that I came here."

"About me, madam?"

"Yes; do not interrupt me! It is so hard
to have a word in private with you—the fates
never favour us now as they used—so I have
taken courage, Juan, and come to you."

"Why courage? You know you are welcome and respected."

"Ah, I am not so sure! But, Juan, you have looked careworn of late, you have confessed to heavy losses, you have hinted at leaving England, and I cannot bear it any longer. If you are in difficulties, let me, out of my abundance, gratify myself by sweeping them away. If you prefer life in England, can *I* not help towards the accomplishment of your wishes? Ah, Juan, I would do much for you!—you know I would!" Lady Helmsford's voice trembled, and nothing save the thought of her rouge would have enabled her to restrain her tears.

"Kind, generous friend," cried Monteiro, drawing a seat beside her and taking her hand in both his own, "your imagination has misled you. I have not lost at play; I am not in difficulties."

"Then what—what is the secret of the change in you? You *know* how changed you are since first we met! Why do you strive to misunderstand all that I would covertly express, until I am compelled to say—'Juan, I faint, I die for your love!' No, no! Let me speak," for he tried to stop her. "I am tortured with doubts. See, Juan, the Countess of Helmsford's husband would have a——"

"Dear lady, I must not, will not hear you ! I will tell you the secret of my preoccupation, and explain *why* I am so situated—I am secretly married."

"Married !" echoed the Countess, growing pale in spite of her rouge. "Juan, why did you not tell me sooner ?"

"Because I was most entangled and hedged in with difficulty."

"Tell me!" cried Lady Helmsford, her bosom heaving with the strong emotion that rent her heart; "is it a marriage you would fain break — that is distasteful?" and she grasped his hand tightly.

"No, by Heaven !" he exclaimed. "If I were but sure that the lady—my wife——" he hesitated.

"Ah !" cried Lady Helmsford, starting to her feet and recoiling from him. "Speak the truth, were it to strike me dead ! A sudden light seems to break upon me. Are you Maud Langley's husband ?"

"I am," returned Monteiro.

Lady Helmsford raised her arms with a sudden despairing gesture. "And you have deceived me! Traitors! both you—and she whom I protected and cherished; preserving her from John Langley and his son for *you*, to destroy myself! Well, sir, they shall have her now, if it was to tear her limb from limb!" And with hasty trembling hands the Countess strove to put on her cloak.

"They shall not," said Monteiro firmly, placing himself between her and the door; "nor shall you go hence in such a mood."

"What!" exclaimed Lady Helmsford, "does it gratify your self-conceit to see my humiliation?"

"You shall not apply such words to yourself in my hearing," he returned, taking her hands and forcing her gently to resume her seat. "In justice to me you must hear what I have to say. I dare not flatter myself that the kindliness you have ever shown me, and which you yourself mistake for a warmer feeling, has really deepened into the seriousness you represent. It is just one of your many whims." He smiled as he spoke.

"As if I did not know," murmured the Countess, soothed by his touch, while bitter, burning tears forced themselves from the darkness of her despairing eyes unnoticed by her.

"You know," he went on rapidly, still holding one hand in a precautionary grasp, "when I met you in Paris I was charmed and fascinated—as most are who come within the range of your influence. I little dreamed then that you were in any way connected with the Langleys—to which family my former beloved chief, Rupert, belonged. I had promised him in his dying moments to befriend Lord Langdale and his child as far as lay in my power. It was the sudden intelligence that a free pardon existed, that John Langley was about to wed the heiress to his son, which roused me to resist the spell you had cast over me. Besides, dear lady, you remember, or perhaps you do not, that you gave me scant encouragement in Paris—that others seemed preferred before me." Lady Helmsford certainly could not remember; but she sat silently listening, her hand in Monteiro's, her bosom heaving, watching to gather some glimpse of hope from his words. "Such was my feeling when I hurriedly, yet reluctantly, quitted Paris," he continued, and proceeded rapidly to sketch the events already recapitulated. "It was in a spirit of mischievous adventure," he concluded, "that I planned the capture and personation of Harold Langley. I never intended to hold Mistress Langley to the species of provisional marriage into which, for her own sake, I was obliged to entrap her. But, dear friend, when I saw this tender, slender girl, helpless in the hands of these cold, cruel, brutal men, a new spirit entered into me—I swore to save her from them!"

The Countess drew her hand from him, shivering with the agony that shot through her, at the indescribable feeling his voice betrayed when he spoke of Maud.

"I returned to London," he went on, "and made arrangements to give up the last ship remaining to me; then I learned your relationship to Mistress Langley, and, I confess, I could not resist the temptation of gazing at the fair girl who was my wife ; but, on my honour, I had most firmly resolved never to let her or any one know the strange tie between us till she was safe and free."

"Then she does not know?" cried Lady Helmsford, giving him her hand once more.

"She does, madam! One unguarded moment betrayed my secret; and since I have been tortured by the sense of duplicity towards you. When I found the King, and the friend on whose interest I counted, were both absent, I had nothing for it but patience and watchfulness. I confess," continued Monteiro, a little reluctantly, for instinct told him he must not confide too entirely in his dear friend, " I had sure traces of the pardon; and I hoped—I do hope when the whole matter is laid before his Majesty, Maud will be placed under proper protection, and freed from all interference from John Langley. This is my tale. I had never meant that Mistress Langley should guess I had stood in the place of her bridegroom; but that night, when I saved her, when she was here, alone in her fear and distress, I could *not* keep back the words ! I claimed the right to comfort and protect her."

A low moan of anguish broke from his hearer. "You were alone ; and she admitted the claim ?"

"No, madam !" cried Monteiro, his cheek reddening; "she shrank from me with such terror as proved to me I hardly knew how to touch a nature so delicate, and made me curse my own impetuosity. Then I prayed her to keep the matter secret, promising that I would never urge any claim upon her ! She implored me to reveal all to you, and only yielded to my entreaties to withhold the knowledge. I thought a few days would end the mystery."

"And you doubted me," interrupted the Countess, "because you knew I loved you ! Better have trusted my generosity than have made a tool of me, Juan, as you have done."

"Nay, dear lady, it is not so."

"It is!" cried Lady Helmsford, breaking from him and pacing the room. "You thought to provide a safe asylum for your wife in the house

of the woman you were betraying, till such time
as it suited you to throw off the mask and show
the world how delicately you had fooled me.
But beware, Juan, lest by your subtlety you
have not made more danger than you have
avoided! Tell me truly, how do matters
stand betwixt you ?"

"Ill for me, madam, Mistress Maud will
not hear me ; and fears me a little less only
than Harold Langley himself."

"Will not hear you! When have you a
chance to speak ?"

"Whenever I can make a chance," exclaimed
Monteiro, infinitely relieved that the terrible
confession was over.

"Treachery all round! You are justly
punished if she does not hear you! and yet
she is most ungrateful, Juan, to you who have
braved so much for her. Ah! Monteiro, con-
trast this coldness with the love I offer ! No
sickly terrors hold me back from the honest
avowal of an affection I would glory in were
it returned !"

Monteiro, with an inexpressible sense of
degradation and discomfort, averted his eyes,

lest they might betray the feeling with which he listened to this comparison of his proud, delicate Maud, with the passionate woman— the heroine, if not much belied, of more than one bold intrigue—who was now humbling herself in the dust before him.

" Her inheritance, too," said the Countess, coming back to her chair, "even if she gains it, is not so great. No doubt some thought of this has somewhat guided you ! And should she gain it, think you the powers that be would let her wed an alien ? Then you say she does not love you ! Oh, Juan ! what a reality you cast aside for the baseless fabric of a dream !" The unhappy woman, leaning her arms on the table, did not attempt to conceal or suppress her sobs.

Monteiro, infinitely distressed and wishing her at Jericho, did all he dared to console and soothe her.

" Tell me," she exclaimed suddenly, " if this fractious girl continues to reject you after you have won her heritage for her, what shall you do ?"

" I know not," he answered sadly. " I shall

then have touched the outside edge of my present world."

"Ah! Monteiro, are you thus infatuated?"

"I cannot account for or control my feelings, dear madam," he cried. "Let me beseech you—be your own noble, generous self. Forgive the error I have been betrayed into by most difficult circumstances. Let me be your true admiring friend—you will soon forget you cared for anything beyond. Continue to protect and cherish my——" he stopped and substituted the words "your niece, at any rate till she is free to make a decision. She loves you and is grateful to you; and she is so young and tender—so innocent of any wilful offence against you—you cannot but love her. Oh, if you will, my utmost devotion, after what I owe my wife, is yours."

"You are an eloquent but not a judicious pleader, Juan," said the Countess scornfully. Then, after a moment's silence and intense rapid thought, in which she reviewed her chances, she went on, "You had better have trusted my generosity from the first."

" I ought, dear Countess, for I am sure your nature is noble."

" Well, well," she replied, turning a little from his gaze, " trust me now. I will deal gently with your—my fanciful niece—and—let me go. I want to recover myself—to be alone. You will come soon, Juan ; you will want to see your wife ?"—bitterly.

" No, madam ; she does not want to see me."

The Countess slowly rose, looking earnestly, passionately at him out of her great dark eyes. " Give me my cloak ; let your man call a chair."

" And you will permit me to accompany you home ?" said Monteiro anxiously, as he wrapped her mantle round her. Her sudden stillness alarmed him.

" No, my friend—my nephew ! I prefer to be alone." She stood silent and motionless for the few moments that intervened before the chair was announced. " Farewell, Juan, perhaps a long farewell. Oh, Juan !" With a sudden impulse she threw her arms round him, resting her head against his shoulder.

It was horribly embarrassing.   As a gallant
gentleman he could not reject a lady's embrace ; but, though holding her kindly for a
moment, he was not in the least tempted to
touch the beautiful rich lips that lay so near
his own.   Availing himself of her slight movement away, he drew her arm through his own
and conducted her to her chair.

"No ; not to St. James's Square," said Lady
Helmsford in a low choking voice ; "to
Madame Hortense, J—— Street."

"May I not come with you ?"

"No, no ; a thousand times no !"

"Victor, follow me," said Monteiro as he
passed his valet after the Countess was
fairly gone ; and he ascended the stairs
rapidly.

To seize his writing-materials, and dash off
a few hurried lines was his first movement on
reaching his room.   These he folded, directed,
and enclosed in another letter containing a
line, and which he directed to Mr. Chifferil.

"Here, Victor," he exclaimed, "take this
to Lady Helmsford's house—you are not

known there—ask for Chifferil; give this into his hand, and return. Speak to none, save to ask for him."

"*Bien*, Monsieur!" said Victor, taking the billet, and departing.

The iron had indeed entered the Countess of Helmsford's soul during the interview just recorded. All the dim forebodings she had scouted as diseased impossible imaginings had been suddenly and hideously realised. Her dreams — the brightest and best she had known perhaps in all her prosperous life— were shattered into a chaotic mass of stinging agony. How was it possible that slight, pallid, insignificant girl could rival *her*—grand and beautiful as she was? but worse than all— than even the sense of having humiliated herself in vain—was the sense of having been made use of by the man she loved, as a convenient protectress for his wife. If it had been *only* a wife, indeed, she would not have so much resented his action; but not all Monteiro's tact and care could hide from her his passionate affection for this proud, shy, cold maiden, who shrank from his love, and trembled at the possibility of his claims.

But if it were so indeed; if Maud was willing and ready to resign him; if it were possible that Juan di Monteiro had neither touched her heart nor her fancy, there was hope yet for herself. Could she persuade Maud to avow her intention to break the marriage, when she had reaped all the benefit she could from it, might not Monteiro's heart yet be caught in the recoil? The game was not quite played out. If Maud was all Monteiro represented her to be, a chance was still left; and Lady Helmsford was not the woman to lose it.

Somewhat calmed by the force of this resolution, the Countess, fearing to meet Maud, compelled herself to dress and take up the iron yoke of social observance. In society she must control herself, and with the exercise of self-control more power would come. She was unusually brilliant and charming; even Lord Chedworth said that had he not been already captivated by the niece, he would have fallen a victim to the aunt.

When at last, thoroughly worn out by the excitement of the day, Lady Helmsford retired to rest, her last order was :

" Tell Chifferil I shall want him in my study to - morrow, early — remember early !"

CHAPTER II.

Y no word or sign did Lady Helmsford betray to her favourite attendant the conflict through which she had passed, or the vague schemes of resistance and revenge that were forming themselves in her brain. She was still and silent from the effects of exhaustion. The only peculiarity which attracted Boville's notice was her mistress's extreme quiet the preceding night and her activity in the morning. Her bell was rung a full hour before her usual time, but she was thoughtful and preoccupied; the only words she spoke during the progress of her toilette were to

ask Beville how she would like to visit Paris again.

"Rarely, my lady!" replied the waiting-woman, who was very proud of being in the train of a lady who thought little of what was then a most wonderful undertaking, *i.e.* a journey to Paris.

"Well, I may go there sooner than you expect. Now, Beville, go to Mistress Langley so soon as you think she is dressed, tell her with—with my *love*, that I hope she rested well, that I fear I cannot see her to-day, that I have no further tidings of Mr. Langley." Lady Helmsford rose as she spoke and walked slowly into her study, or boudoir. Chifferil had not yet made his appearance, and the Countess sat down at her writing-table, murmuring to herself; "No, I must not see her yet! I must put matters in train first," took pen and paper, but sat some time in deep thought without using either.

Whatever the success of the plan she was striving to mature, a visit to Paris was the best sort of retreat she could secure. If Maud, yielding to her aunt's suggestion,

wrote to claim Monteiro's promise to set her
free, declaring her own determination not to
confirm the ceremony through which they had
gone—good! Lady Helmsford would then
really rouse herself and set to work in earnest
to deliver her from Langley—would protect
and provide for her! Then to the Countess
would be the gracious task of consoling
Monteiro, and obliterating from his mind all
thought of the insipid child he chose to call
his wife! Even then Paris would be a safer
scene of reparation and reconciliation than
London. If Maud was so base and treacherous
as to hold Monteiro to his vows, and her
own——but no! Lady Helmsford had not
the courage just then to face this alternative,
still less to let the desperate cruel purpose,
she knew was exhaling from the volcano of
her heart, form itself visibly before her mental
vision. No, at this stage of thought she
shrunk somewhat from that of which, under
certain conditions, she knew she was capable.
If, however, her best hopes were fulfilled, it
was of the last importance that Monteiro's
marriage with Maud should be kept a pro-

found secret. It would be a delightful morsel of scandal for gossip, her espousals with a man who had already gone through were it merely the wedding ceremony with her niece ! Yes—to Paris she would go. At last she dipped her pen in the ink, and wrote slowly and carefully for a while. She had already folded and directed the letter, when Chifferil entered with an air of haste and some confusion.

" Pardon me, my lady, I had no idea you would be so early !"

" I *said* early !" replied the Countess sharply. " But no excuses—let me see your accounts." For more than half-an-hour did this woman, so lately overwhelmed and blinded by her passionate infatuation for Monteiro, look narrowly into her affairs, asking sudden questions, and acquainting herself with all details since her last recent examination ; she paused at length. " You are a good accountant, Chifferil, and a useful servant," she said ; " I am about to show my confidence in you, but first tell me how you came to know Don Monteiro so well." She spoke with a careless assurance of the fact, which overthrew the small degree of self-possession possessed by Chifferil. He was fearfully embarrassed. What did she or did she not know? How much ought he to tell her? had Don Monteiro revealed the fact of his devotion to Lord Langdale's daughter, which even Chifferil began to suspect was more than obedience to the wishes of his defunct commander, or revenge on John Langley?

"Don Monteiro—madam—my lady," he hesitated.

"Is your head still confused," she asked scornfully, "that you cannot understand so simple a question? How came you to know the Don so well?"

"I do not know him so very well, madam. I—you remember I met the gentleman in Paris, with your ladyship, and he was good enough to converse with me at times——"

"Yes, yes," cried Lady Helmsford; "but when did you enter into a league together touching Mistress Langley?" The Countess in thus speaking fired a bold random shot.

" Mistress Maud Langley ! your ladyship
—I—a——"

" Come, man ! speak truly ; don't go into a
fit, striving to frame improbable lies ! Do
you think I shall be angry with you for
helping Don Monteiro to befriend my niece ?
only you might both have trusted *me*
more !"

" Indeed, madam," cried Chifferil, somewhat reassured both by her tone and words,
" I was most ready to do my utmost for the
young lady ! You see I was not unknown to
the late lord, I was indeed under deep obligations to him ; but knowing, that is hearing,
that no very great friendship existed between
your ladyship and——"

" In short," she interrupted him, " that
Langdale and I hated each other as only near
connections do—go on, Chifferil."

" I did not think necessary to acquaint
your ladyship."

" When did you learn that Monteiro was
also interested in Lord Langdale ?"

" I see your ladyship knows all ! Has the
Don told you ?"

" He has—be quick !—speak !"

" Well then, madam, hearing that my lord
was sick and ill, I ventured, when in Paris,
to find his lodgings and ask after him. After
he had breathed his last, I met Don Juan,
bound on the same errand as myself; we then
spoke together, and I promised to let him
know what I found out respecting the young
orphan ; he made the same promise to me. I
took occasion afterwards to mention the—the
enmity that existed between my lord and
your ladyship."

" Indeed !" cried Lady Helmsford. "This
may in a measure account—" then interrupt-
ing herself : " What did he tell you of the
strange wedding ?"

" Nothing, madam, save that he was very
fearful the impostor, whoever he might be,
should molest the young lady. He knows no
more of it than we do !"

" Ha ! you think so !" said the Countess,
giving him a piercing look. She was silent
for a few seconds.

Chifferil then knew nothing of this detest-
able unfortunate marriage, that was good so

far. In fact Chifferil knew very little ; still, he was too much of a partisan for Maud to be permitted access to either her or that maddening, fascinating Juan.

"Enough about Mistress Maud and her affairs," said Lady Helmsford, rousing herself from her thoughts. "Attend to the commission I am about to give you ; I said I would prove my appreciation of your services. I have for some time been dissatisfied with Hawkshaw, my agent at Helmsford ; he seems to have been reducing rents and felling trees somewhat recklessly. I want you to go down suddenly, without previous warning, examine his accounts, see to the condition of house and land and tenants, see also if it might not be made a suitable residence for my niece should she wish to retire there, make yourself acquainted with everything and report to me. Here," handing him the letter she had just finished, "here is your authority ; see you start to-morrow morning ; send to-night and secure your place in the stage coach. I will write a cheque for your expenses and a quarter's salary in advance,

which shall be in addition to your usual pay.
You may leave me now, for you have, no doubt,
preparations to make."

"But, my lady!" cried the wretched
Chifferil, to whom a journey into Yorkshire
was a labour of Hercules, and to whose
imagination the dangers of the north road
arrayed themselves in awful magnitude,
"this is indeed sudden and unexpected;
moreover 'tis a toilsome journey, I——"

"Do you hesitate?" cried my lady. "If
you are too dainty and fearful to carry out
my instructions readily and with energy,
quit my service! I cannot be impeded by
drones. Are you willing to start to-morrow
or not?"

"Of course, madam, I am," said Chifferil
despairingly, for he had no idea of resigning
his excellent appointment.

"Very well; leave me now, I shall see you
again this evening."

Soon after, her ladyship's carriage was
ordered, and she proceeded to execute a large
amount of business; she visited my Lord
Sunderland at the Treasury, her stock-broker

in Change Alley, her lawyer in Gray's Inn, besides sundry shops and various fine ladies.

As she drove homewards down Pall Mall, she espied the chariot of Lord Chedworth, who, with courteous gesticulations, motioned to her coachman to stop, then descended and addressed her ladyship through the carriage window, hat in hand.

"I am but now returned lamenting from your ladyship's mansion. The fair châtelaine was abroad, the gentle Mistress Maud indisposed and invisible! Permit me, madam, to entreat you will alight, and honour me by taking a turn on the Mall. 'Tis beauteous weather, and the *beau monde* is all assembled. Suffer me to present my arm."

"Thank you, my lord, I will accept your obliging offer," returned Lady Helmsford, and disengaging her hoop she contrived to squeeze it through the door less ungracefully than most women.

The carriages had met near Spring Gardens, and Lord Chedworth conducted her ladyship with elaborate politeness into the park. It was a beautiful day, more like April than the

end of February, and the fashionable promenade
was crowded. Hoop met hoop, and gallants
entangled their rapiers in draperies. Many
and varied were the gorgeous costumes and
rich braveries of both men and women. Lady
Helmsford was well employed acknowledging
this acquaintance, and bowing to that, yet
did her large eager eyes not fail to seek for
one well-known figure, yet in vain. She had
thought it not unlikely that Don Juan might
have been among the fashionable crowd when
she accepted Lord Chedworth's invitation to
walk ; but he was nowhere to be seen. Next
a jealous pang shot through her ; was it
possible that while she was searching for him
in the crowd he had taken advantage of her
absence, and was perhaps even now pleading
his cause with Maud—and not in vain ? Lady
Helmsford could *not* imagine Monteiro pleading in vain ; but she *could* imagine, with
maddening distinctness, how such a man as
Juan would avail himself of the curious link
that existed between him and the woman he
sought. These ideas made her feverish, and
very inattentive to her companion's polite

conversation; at length, just as she was about to say she would leave the Mall, her intention was arrested by the mention of Maud.

" I regret to find sweet Mistress Langley is not so well! Methought she seemed wonderfully restored when I had the pleasure of seeing her the other evening. Ah, madam! I fear me your friendship is scarce so stanch as I had hoped, or you would have granted me ere this opportunity to plead my suit personally to your fair niece. Certes, her position is painful, and I so far agree with her ignoble guardian, that the best way to neutralise the fictitious marriage, is by substituting a real one. I think if I could represent to the young lady the ease, security, and affection her marriage with myself would ensure, she might be induced to overlook the disparity of our years and my small merit !"

" My dear lord !" cried Lady Helmsford, " she would be a most fortunate woman were she to become your wife! You know you have my best wishes! let me think; you shall have the opportunity you wish for to-

morrow or next day. John Langley threatens
to remove her from me, and a more favourable
moment could not be found. I do think the
poor child likes you well, but she has been so
grievously tormented she has scarce a chance
of knowing what she really does like. To-
morrow, or if I find it more advisable, the
next day, I will send you a little note appoint-
ing an hour when you shall see Maud alone,
nor do I doubt so skilled a gallant as Lord
Chedworth will know how to make his suit
acceptable."

She smiled encouragingly on the gallant
old nobleman, thinking the while, " If I can
pique or coerce Maud into wedding him, my
game is half won."

"Good-day, dear Lady Helmsford !" cried
Mistress Ferrars, stopping them. " Why, it
is a marvel to see you among the herd of
ordinary mortals in the Mall ! you seldom
deign to honour the promenade ! My Lord
Chedworth, how goes on your search ? Have
you tracked the villains who sought to carry
off Mistress Langley, yet ?"

The pretty Mistress Ferrars was accompanied by Sir Eustace Blount and a following of other beaux, suitable to her standing as a belle.

" Alas !" said Lord Chedworth, " I have had but scant success, a poor postillion and a stable-man are all we have lit upon. The larger game have escaped."

After a little desultory conversation and remarks on the news of the day, Sir Eustace observed :

" His Majesty has been wondrously favoured by winds and tides. He landed last evening at Dover."

" Last night ! what fairy has told you ?" cried Lady Helmsford. " Why, 'tis scarce five o'clock now !"

" It is a fact, nevertheless," returned Sir Eustace conceitedly ; " though not yet generally known. I happened to pass the Treasury not twenty minutes ago, and met Craggs ; we stopped to speak, while so doing, up came a horseman, disordered by hard riding. 'Ha!' says Craggs, 'an express from Dover ! I fancy the King is landed.' He left me ; I made inquiry and was told the conjecture was true."

"Then he will be here on Wednesday at furthest," said Lord Chedworth.

"Oh, sooner! I say Tuesday!" exclaimed one.

"No, no! Thursday is about the mark!" and so on, each naming a different day; the younger men backing their opinions with wagers of various amounts.

On Lady Helmsford the tidings produced a strong effect. The plot was thickening; what she had to do she must do quickly. Yet she scarce acknowledged to herself that, with all her daring, she shrank from the scene with Maud which was before her. Not that she hated giving her pain, though to this she was not quite indifferent, but the picture of Maud blushing for her when she boldly confessed her love for Monteiro, the tender shame she knew that proud yet simple girl would feel at such an avowal, made her turn hot and cowardly; but it must be done. Nothing else would touch Maud so much; terrible as the price would be, costly in the depth of self-abasement into which she must voluntarily descend, she would pay it, even

to the uttermost farthing, rather than renounce the delightful dreams which had
brought back to her world-beaten heart
something of youth's delicious freshness.
The King's return would enable Monteiro to
bring matters to a crisis, for she felt, rather
than thought, that he had revealed his plans
to her, but partially so ; to-morrow—ay—to-
morrow she would decide Maud's fate.

" I am somewhat weary, Lord Chedworth ;
be so good as to call my carriage and my
people," exclaimed the Countess, starting from
her thoughts.

It was the morning of the following day.
Maud was reading some numbers of the
Spectator, which her residence in France
had hitherto prevented her from enjoying.
Dorothy was busy at her needle, glad to see
her dear lady so much better as to read on
quietly, for she had been terribly restless of
late.

" And has the Countess not asked for me ?"
said Maud, looking up from her book. " Why,
'tis nearly three days since I have seen her."

"Well! she used oftener to be four nor three," said Dorothy soothingly.

"Yet it is very strange and distressing," murmured Maud, drawing from her pocket an oft-conned note which had reached her in the afternoon of the day on which her aunt had visited Monteiro, and seeing Dorothy absorbed in her stitchery, she read it once more:

"I have done your bidding, dearest cousin and wife—forgive the word! I cannot erase it! The Countess now knows all my devotion to you—knows that I am the mysterious bridegroom; but I have thought it wiser not to reveal my true name and station; let this be a guide to you. Let *nothing* persuade you to renounce me till we can once more speak together. Be brave and patient yet a little while, and, in any case, all will be well for you!

"Ever your loving servant and husband,
                "RUPERT L——."

The Countess knew all! and yet had sought

no explanation with herself! Maud could not understand it ; reason with herself as she would, the absence of all demonstration seemed terribly ominous. If Lady Helmsford was angry, why did she not come and express her anger with her usual impetuosity? if her anger was so deep as to need regulating and concealment, Maud felt indeed as if she were but in the beginning of troubles. In preparation for such a possibility she approached the fire, and committed the note to the flames. It was strange that, in spite of his promises to set her free—to make no attempt to uphold the marriage, which indeed he could not—her cousin Rupert persisted in signing himself her "husband." It was scarcely right of him, though of course it would be of little importance. Would he be successful in winning her inheritance for her ? and if so—or, indeed, if not—how could she show her gratitude for his great devotion to her ? which was none the less precious in her sight because she thought some—a good deal —of it was due to regard for her dead father. But all these considerations were dwarfed by

the immense uneasiness caused by Lady
Helmsford's silence and non-appearance.
Thus thinking, she knelt still by the fire,
and was almost startled into a scream by a
tap at the door.

"Come in," she said faintly.

It opened to admit the slim, affected little
figure of Mistress Letitia Sparrow, who came
nominally to ask after Maud—really to relieve
her mind by a little gossip with Dorothy.

"Well, I am sure I do not know what is
going to happen," she exclaimed, after the
polite preliminaries were duly performed.
"What do you think?"

Maud's heart beat with apprehension; but
Dorothy, who was a little cross from the long
spell of seclusion she had lately endured, and
had just at that moment a difficulty in thread-
ing her needle, said a little dryly:

"Oh! you may as well tell at once; I
haven't the ghost of a thought left in me."

"Dear Mistress Dorothy! you are always
so bright," returned Mistress Sparrow, with
her head on one side. "Well! do you know!
my lady has sent off Mr. Chifferil all the way

to Yorkshire! The poor man started this morning; and terribly loath was he to go such a long dangerous journey. He was up half the night, Mr. Hobson has been telling me, making his will, and such like."

"Oh! bless us and save us! what's that for?" said Dorothy, laying down her work.

"Does my aunt not usually send him on such errands?" asked Maud, struck by the remembrance that Chifferil had evidently been an ally of Monteiro's.

"I never knew her despatch him to Helmsford, or indeed anywhere far away, before; I think her ladyship cannot be well; she was up and doing so wondrous early this morning."

"Faith, you are a wonderful set of people," exclaimed Dorothy; "when you are well and hearty you lie in bed, and when you are 'indisposed,' as you call it, you get up at cockcrow."

"Why do you think my aunt is unwell?"

"Because, sweet Mistress Langley, as I was going into her room this morning, that impertinent upsetting person, Mistress Beville, was coming out; so she said—'You needn't trouble to go in, Mistress Sparrow,' says she; 'my lady is not very well; she has been up this hour and more,' she says, 'and very much engaged, so she doesn't want you.'"

"I think that Mistress Beville wouldn't mind saying more than her prayers," said Dorothy sagely.

"I fear me much she does not say many prayers," replied Mistress Sparrow, shaking her head with disapprobation.

"But there is no doubt my lady has been monstrous busy writing a quantity without any help; and the green chariot and greys were in the city yesterday, so Thomas told Cicely, the second housemaid. I feel a sort of all-overness myself, as if something was going to happen—I do not know what."

"Dear heart, no!" cried Dorothy.

"Why do you think so?" asked Maud gently; "Lady Helmsford is generally much occupied."

"Ay! dear lady; but she would go no-where last night : she sat at home and alone the whole evening. Moreover, there was to have been a reception and card-party on Tuesday, and part of poor Chifferil's work yestereven was writing notes to put it off."

" Well, I fear we can but believe Lady Helmsford is really ill, in spite of her early rising—I trust it is not so," cried Maud, a sensation of dread creeping gradually over her heart. "Why should I not go and ask?" she continued, restlessly rising and moving towards the door. "None are so near of kin, after mother and daughter, as aunt and niece, and yet we are almost strangers."

" I pray you, my dear young lady, do not so," cried Letitia ; "my lady does not like to be thought ill, or to want care ; she would, perhaps, repulse you."

" Set her up," said Dorothy, with an air of scorn ; " she ought to be proud to have such a niece : and what is she, to be different from the rest of the poor creatures about her ! Ah ! God help us ! It's well there are eyes so far above us, that the difference between high and low must seem small indeed."

" Anyway," concluded Mistress Sparrow, " I never knew my lady in quite such a way before.

41—2

I did speak to her for a few minutes in the
boudoir this morning, as I wished to tell her
poor little Mab would not eat her breakfast—
but she did not heed me; and as Mr. Harvey,
the solicitor, was announced just then, I came
away.   I have, therefore, acted to the best of
my judgment respecting Mab, and I trust it
will *prove* for the best."

"I'm sure *I* do, for your own sake as well
as for the little brute's," cried Dorothy.

Maud, too much disturbed by Mistress
Letitia's conjectures, as well as too polite to
read, took up her embroidery, as an excuse
for thinking.   All that she had heard made
her aunt's avoidance of her more threatening.
She feared she had offended past reconciliation by concealing her knowledge of Monteiro's identity: yet she could not blame
herself for being guided by him in a matter
he evidently thought of so much importance.

Still, was it not cowardly in her not to go
down boldly and face her aunt? She had done
nothing wrong; she——

"My lady the Countess wishes to speak

with Mistress Langley in her dressing-room immediately," said one of the footmen, opening the door, after having tapped for admittance.

"Goodness preserve us! you've taken away my breath," cried Letitia.

Maud rose silently, and crossing to Dorothy, kissed her brow, as if she was herself going to execution, then without a word followed the servant who had summoned her.

Dorothy looked after her and shook her head.

"Ah! my darlin', you are too young to be so fretted!" she exclaimed.

CHAPTER III.

LADY HELMSFORD had been apparently pacing the room when Maud
entered. She was still in her *robe
de chambre*—deadly pale—her hair
turned back from her face in a loose wavy
mass. She stood still when Maud entered,
and kept silence even after the door was
securely closed upon them both. Something,
she knew not what, save that she *felt* it was
hatred, gleamed in the stern eyes fixed upon
her by her aunt.

"You have been ill!" cried Maud, fearful of
waiting longer in silence. "You are still unwell! why did you not send for me before?"

"So! Maud Langley," said Lady Helmsford, speaking slowly, and never moving her eyes from the face that flushed nervously beneath them, "you have found your bridegroom; you are the wife of Juan di Monteiro!"

"No! madam," returned Maud, gathering courage now the awful silence was broken; "I do not consider myself his wife; the ceremony which we went through is not binding on either."

"How long have you known he was your bridegroom?"

"Since the night he rescued me."

"Over ten days! ten days and nights you have enjoyed the safe shelter of my roof—you have eaten of my bread and drank of my cup—and hidden this thing from me!" said Lady Helmsford bitterly—contemptuously.

"Indeed, dear aunt, it was ill done; and I was miserable until you knew all." Maud stopped abruptly, too loyal to clear herself by blaming another. "I—that is we—thought it wiser to keep the matter entirely secret—"

"*We,*" interrupted Lady Helmsford, with

suppressed fury, "we! Do you assume the conjugal style already? This does not tally with your declaration that you do not consider yourself his wife."

"Madam," said Maud, endeavouring to take her hand, "I have done wrong in concealing my knowledge from you for an hour; but be generous! forgive me! at least the matter was voluntarily revealed to you."

"Ah! Do you know *how* it was revealed?" asked the Countess, her cheeks growing crimson.

"No, dear aunt; I only know I implored Monsieur di Monteiro to tell you, and he has done so."

"Stand back, traitress! do not touch me! You implored Monteiro! Where did you meet this husband whom you do not mean to acknowledge?—beware, girl! one meeting without witnesses might suffice to rivet your chains with a man even of ordinary honour, if he cared to do so."

Maud's colour left her cheek so visibly at these words that the Countess saw, and determined to profit by, the terror she had created.

" Indeed, madam, I only spoke to him here —in this house—only a few words; and I think he is too truly a man of honour to break the promise he has given to hold me free."

" He has promised you this," said Lady Helmsford, looking at her keenly, and forgetting in the hope it suggested to ask further as to the meeting. " Come, Maud—I have been deeply and sorely hurt at the want of confidence you have shown; so deeply, that for a whole day I have not trusted myself to see or speak to you. Now sit down; I will try to forgive you—and let us see what is best to be done."

" Oh, thank you ; you are indeed good to me, dear aunt," cried Maud ; " I shall gladly follow your advice—for you are wise as well as good."

Lady Helmsford was silent for a few minutes. " Maud," she said at length, " I see you are in a position of great difficulty : your marriage with Monteiro must be kept

the most profound secret. If John Langley
knew of it! He would go any lengths of
cruelty and outrage to compel you to be his
son's wife. So far, Monteiro is right. You
say you are anxious to be freed from this
temporary marriage ; is this truth ?"

"It is, madam," said Maud faintly.

"You are wise," returned Lady Helmsford,
still keeping her stern eyes fastened on Maud's
face ; "because we must remember that however honourable Monteiro may be, he is a
stranger, of whose resources we know nothing.
He has some scheme in his head which, if
it succeeds, will make you a rich prize—and
then he proposes to turn this phantom of a
marriage into a real one. Maud, this man
has told you of his love !"

"He has," she replied, her colour returning
with a vivid blush.

Lady Helmsford flung aside the hand she
held, with an angry gesture. "And you believed him ?"

"Alas ! madam, 'tis hard to know what to
believe ; but he *seemed* in earnest."

This time a smile lurked round the lips

that spoke, and with the downcast eyes and blushing cheek made so sweet a picture that Lady Helmsford rose with a muttered exclamation, turned from her, walked down the room and back to her seat before she spoke again. " Ay ! he did not *seem* in earnest for the first time, I'll warrant ; he has sworn the same love to *me*—to fifty others."

" I suppose so," returned Maud quietly, a certain scene returning to her mind, as well as Monteiro's emphatic assertion that he had never sought Lady Helmsford ; yet she was not quite able to forget the expression of his earnest pleading eyes and imploring accents.

" You suppose so !" repeated the Countess. " Are you then really indifferent to him ? Speak ! Maud, speak !"

" Indeed, madam, I am not indifferent to one who has so truly served and saved me ; but you do not suppose I could love—really love, give my whole heart to so great a stranger—one whom you, who know him so much better, think scarce deserving of belief."

" How incomprehensible to me is this halting between two moods !" cried the Countess. "Then do you believe the love he professes ?"

"Not so much as in his real wish to befriend me," cried Maud; "I might believe in his affection did I not think that—that you perhaps liked—that is cared for him; and who would look at me when *you* were kind——"

Maud spoke with downcast eyes, as though confessing some shame of her own, yet with sincere conviction of her aunt's superiority.

Lady Helmsford hesitated : should she bare the bruises of her pride to this insignificant inexperienced girl! should she show herself less than her listener in dignity and self-control! for in her heart she did not doubt that Monteiro had lavished all the passionate eloquence of which he was master upon the simple maiden he had a sort of right to call his wife : yet *she* had kept her judgment clear. No! this was an additional humiliation the Countess could not brook. She would *not* confess her weakness; and by this distrust of Maud's nobility and generosity she lost the game. She laughed scornfully.

"*I* care for Monteiro! Yes! as I care for those that give some charm to the passing hour; his admiration amused me; his character interested me! But I know him, and do not wish to see you deceived. Maud, be ruled by me—make me your friend. Write a letter to Monteiro! tell him you are pained by the ambiguous situation in which you find yourself; ask him to send you a written renunciation of his possible rights; tell him of your gratitude, offer him an ample reward when he shall have gained you your lands—I will help you to express it, though he must *never* know I did so,—and—and—Maud! if you will do this—if you will be guided by me, I will be your friend, your sister, your mother—but you must obey,—here—here is the paper—the pen."

With feverish eagerness the Countess placed writing materials before Maud, who was shocked and startled by the vehemence her aunt could not suppress.

"You know," she continued, "however much I may like the amusement of Monteiro's society, we cannot deny that he is a species of

adventurer—one knows not who ; and I ought
not to encourage any love passages between
you ; but you will write, child ?"

" No, aunt," said Maud, drawing back, "it
is unnecessary ; I so far trust this gentleman
as to believe his promise that he will not
attempt to claim me. If he should be disposed to break it—why, you all tell me he
cannot enforce this marriage ; besides I would
not for worlds offend him with any offer of
reward. Why write or make any motion ?
let him carry out his plan, whatever it may
be ; 'twill be time enough to act after."

" Maud !" cried Lady Helmsford, " you love
this man ! Listen to me : if you do not write
as I dictate I shall not feel justified in keeping you here. I have already resisted John
Langley's claim to your custody, and the
responsibility of protecting you is more than
I care to undertake. Should Monteiro carry
you off, or, more likely, persuade you to go
with him, I should be held accountable."

" Indeed, madam," exclaimed Maud indignantly, " you wrong Monsieur di Monteiro
—he would disdain to do either !"

"Ha! you say so! Dare you look in my eyes and say he has not already tried?" cried the Countess fiercely: and Maud, recalling his first passionate outburst, stood convicted and covered with confusion.

" 'Twas only for a moment he forgot himself," she cried, "and, in truth, I was so frightened I scarce remember anything distinctly; but oh! aunt! whatever my errors may be—and I cannot see in what I have sinned—do not terrify me by a threat of restoring me to my guardian."

She wrung her hands, and in spite of her brave efforts for self-control, the tears would come.

" Do not—do not!" she sobbed.

" Write!" said Lady Helmsford, "and you need fear nothing! Write! and I will shelter you from all molestation; but once let this matter reach John Langley's ears, he will seize you, and murder Monteiro. Come, give yourself a respite from all this misery: if you are indifferent to this man, write! or quit my house and seek shelter where you may!"

The words had scarce left Lady Helmsford's lips before she saw that the fulfilment of such a threat would only serve to drive her niece into the shelter of Monteiro's protection : she burned to recall them—especially as Maud, roused into self-possession, suddenly raised her head, which she had bent down on her hands, and looking steadily at her aunt, said gravely and firmly :

"Lady Helmsford, you are unjust. I have done nothing to deserve such threats; 'tis no fault of mine that Monsieur di Monteiro sought to save me, for my father's sake, by the only means in his power. Why are you thus enraged, madam ? I never dreamed of rivalry with you; if you think Monteiro has been false to you, do you imagine I would accept a forsworn husband ?"

"Insolent girl !" cried the Countess, stung by the sense of superior strength these words —unconsciously to the speaker—conveyed, "how dare you speak to me of rivalry ! *you* a rival ! *you* refuse to accept Monteiro ! I believe you are more deeply committed to him than you dare acknowledge ; I gather from your speech that you have seen him oftener than I know ; your refusal to write, in accordance with your own professions, all prove to me that Monteiro and yourself have been fooling me with some devilish half revelation. I will know the whole truth ; I will cross-examine your confidante—your complaisant duenna !" She darted to the bell as she spoke and rang it violently.

"Mistress Langley's woman ! send her directly !" she exclaimed to the servant, who came in haste.

"She can tell but little," said Maud, still upheld by the indignation her aunt had roused ; "I have told her nothing. Believe me, madam, the wisest course for us all is faith and patience. There is no need for this anger with me. The promise I have given to Monsieur di Monteiro I will keep."

"What promise ? what ?" said Lady Helmsford from between her closed teeth.

"That I would trust his word, keep the secret, and wait his time for unravelling the mystery."

This evidence of the good understanding

between Maud and her lover-husband finished
the perturbation and rage of the Countess.
Maud's affectation of indifference then was a
mere blind. Her firm refusal to write as the
Countess dictated, a proof of her resolution
not to break with Monteiro.

"Come here, woman!" cried Lady Helmsford to Dorothy, who entered, and, after
dropping a deep curtsy, stood at the door;
"come here, and tell me what you know of
this marriage."

Dorothy, alarmed at the voice and look of
her interrogator, glanced at the tearful,
agitated countenance of her young mistress,
and prepared herself to avoid all admis-
sions.

"Sure, I have told you all about it before,
my lady."

"No! you have not told me the bridegroom's name."

"Why, that's what we all want to find out,
my lady."

"Woman! take care how you prevaricate.
Do you mean to say your mistress has not
told you?"

"Ah! how could she? sure she doesn't know herself."

"You are a good actress, Mistress Dorothy; nevertheless, I believe you know as well as I do that she is wedded to Monteiro."

"Oh! blessed hour!" cried Dorothy, clasping her hands together in the blankest astonishment, "you don't say so! Oh! isn't he an illigant gentleman! and what is he in his own country, my lady? a lord or a duke?"

"How can I know what to believe!" cried Lady Helmsford. "Tell me, you maddening creature! where, and how, did he gain access to your lady?"

"Oh! faith, my lady, he never did; unless, indeed, 'twas when he took her from those thieves of the world. Sure I have been with her day and night, and I will take my oath she never spoke to mortal in my hearing. If she saw him at all it was when he was taking tay with your ladyship."

"Heaven only knows if you are speaking truth or falsehood. My head turns."

"Ah, my jewel! what is the matter at all, at all?" cried Dorothy, turning to Maud.

"My aunt is much disturbed; she thinks Monsieur di Monteiro an unsuitable partner for me; and I refuse to make any step towards disengaging myself from him, because it is wiser and more just to trust him."

"Trust him!" cried Lady Helmsford; "a reckless adventurer! a man to whom women are toys to be deceived and cast aside—who——"

"Oh! the villain!" interrupted Dorothy, making a slight grimace to Maud, unseen by the Countess; "I am sure you ought to be obliged to my lady for telling you the truth. See, my lady, she looks as white as a ghost, and her eyes full of tears: hadn't she better come upstairs with me, and you just write—write what you think best——"

"I do not agree to that," murmured Maud.

"Go; leave us!" said the Countess more calmly, seeing that she could do nothing with Dorothy—that she was rather a support than otherwise to her mistress ; " Mistress Langley will join you in a few moments."

" Hear me, Maud," she continued when they were again alone, motioning her to a seat; " I have been harsh and hasty, but I fear for your future, child. If you think that you are so bound by your promise to Monteiro, let me write to him ; I will do so kindly and clearly, and then I shall feel justified in keeping the matter from John Langley. In truth, Maud, I love you—I only love not contradiction. Moreover, I have promised Lord Chedworth that he should see you to-day or to-morrow. Oh, Maud, there is your real chance of safety, happiness, rank, distinction ! He is splendid in his liberality, charming in conversation, devoted to you ! let him plead his own cause."

" No, no, my aunt," said Maud, smiling, her suspicions of Lady Helmsford's motives now thoroughly awoke ; " I will not subject that good nobleman to the unnecessary mortification of a personal rejection. What ! with the chance (for I believe there is one) of being in a few days rich, free, the world

before me, the possibility of finding a partner
of my own age and mind, shall I tie myself to a man, kind and pleasant, no doubt,
lovable as a father, but not so as a husband?
'twould be but scant courage that would buy
a few days' security at so high a price. I will
dare what a week may bring forth; there is
no need to take either Lord Chedworth or
Monsieur di Monteiro at the end of it."

"Enough!" exclaimed Lady Helmsford.
"This is defiance! 'Tis the ordinary run of
gratitude. Leave me."

"No, not while you think me ungrateful!"
cried Maud, taking her hand in spite of her
aunt's efforts to withhold it. "You are unhappy and disturbed; you are unlike yourself.
Be just, be generous. I would fain love you
—why will you not let me?"

"Love me! You!—you, who have robbed
me and turned my blood to gall! Go!—
speak no more. Leave me, while I can restrain myself. Go! consider yourself a prisoner till I decide what to do." With a
gesture of disdain and dismissal Lady Helmsford turned from her and again rang.

Maud, feeling that any further appeal was useless, left the room.

"Oh, Dorothy—dear Dorothy! do you forgive me for not telling you everything?" cried Maud, throwing her arms round the faithful creature's neck. "But I had promised——"

"Faith, I'll forgive you that fast enough! but what I will not forgive is for going and telling my lady!—she that's ready to ate him. Ah, what made ye do it at all, at all?"

"It was only right, Dorothy; I ought not to deceive her."

"Ah, then it's sorrow we'll sup for your right doing. Who's there?"

"Only Beville, Mistress Dorothy."

"Oh! walk in, ma'am." (*Sotto voce*) "What mischief is she after?"

"I beg pardon, madam," said the waiting-woman, curtsying with a stolid, set expression of face, "but my lady wishes the key of your chamber."

Without waiting for a reply she took it, curtsied again, and retreated. The next moment they heard it turn sharply in the lock, and knew they were prisoners.

"Well, if that is not a dirty trick I never saw one!" cried Dorothy. "Let me go, darlin'; there is another door out of the bedroom leads on to the back stairs—let me take the key out of that."

"'Tis useless, Dorothy," said Maud sadly. "Do you not think another would soon be found? We are in the Countess of Helmsford's hands; she must do as seems best to her."

"And bad will be that best," cried Dorothy, hastening away just in time to hear the sharp click of the second bolt as it was shot from outside.

"God forgive you, my Lady Helmsford," said Dorothy, trembling with fury, "for a revengeful, unwomanly devil! I will see if I can't circumvent ye! Faith now! the windies is half way up to the moon, and the chimbley's mighty narrow. Ah! if one had a dawshy bit of a chimbley-boy, like Gomez, now! that Nature blacked as if a purpose to mock the soot."

"Is it locked too?" cried Maud, coming behind her. "It is too bad—too insulting. I feel too angry to be frightened now. But oh!

pray God she may not send me back to John Langley !"

The evening after this stormy interview, Monteiro had returned from a visit to old Robilliard. He was extremely restless and uneasy at having heard nothing from Lady Helmsford. The silence and inaction of that lady seemed to him an evil omen; besides, it was several days since he had seen Maud, and the pathos of her voice as she said, " Rupert, you are very good to me," still haunted his heart. What if Lady Helmsford had employed the time which intervened since their last interview in poisoning Maud's mind! She might tell some tales that would sound strange to a young, imaginative, delicate girl; but she might invent far worse. With all her passion and self-will, there was a certain amount of nobility and generosity in Lady Helmsford which inspired Monteiro with the hope that at least she would not be false. If he could but convert this proud, masterful woman into a friend, all might go well so far as Maud's safety was concerned; beyond this at present he must not look.

Entering his lodgings somewhat cast down, he found a man in a mulberry-coloured livery awaiting him.

" A letter, sir, from Sir Stephen Compton," said the messenger.

To seize and tear it open was the work of a moment.

" My DEAR SIR,"—it ran—" I arrived here safely (although my bones still ache) yester even. I would be much gratified if you could breakfast with me by ten o'clock to-morrow ; I have much to do, and that is my most leisure time. I have good tidings, but they must keep. Let me have a reply by the hand of the bearer.

" I am, dear sir,
" Your obliged and obedient servant,
" STEPHEN COMPTON."

Monteiro quickly penned a grateful reply, and then, throwing himself into an easy-chair, gave himself to reflection, not untinged with sadness, although satisfaction predominated. That he would defeat John Langley's schemes he felt tolerably sure. That he would also win Maud's lands and rank for her he did not doubt ; but after ! how would it be with himself ?—either bliss or woe.

If she was still averse to him, or if that dangerous, uncertain woman, Lady Helmsford, had employed the ample time at her disposal in poisoning Maud's mind against him, he could never sue to the wealthy heiress as he could have done to the penniless orphan. In fact the decision was now in her hands ; a few days—nay, a few hours perhaps—would proclaim her Baroness Langdale, mistress of a noble fortune. He was bound to resign his shadowy claim to be her husband, and to enrol himself amid the many pretenders to her hand who would soon spring up, with less advantage than the rest, in that he was poor and known to have strange adventurous antecedents. True he had been fortunate in being able to serve her ; but he rejected indignantly the idea of gratitude or reward. He yearned for her whole unreserved heart ; he burned to read tenderness in her soft, dark-blue eyes, to feel love in the lingering touch of her slender hand, to hear the clear tones of the voice that was music to *him* speak in the full confidence of trust and affection, to find the sweet, pensive, sensitive mouth given frankly, willingly to his kisses. But how slight was his chance of ever reaching such a heaven! The only faint gleam of hope that visited him was the memory of her accent and words when they last parted.

What was she doing now? Why might he not at least make an attempt to see her? He rose with this intention, and had opened the door to summon his valet, when he made his appearance ushering in Gomez.

Never was a little negro more warmly welcomed. Monteiro at first thought he must be sent by Maud, but he was soon undeceived. With many grins and duckings of the head Gomez produced a letter in Lady Helmsford's writing.

"Take him and feed him, Victor," said Monteiro; "bring him to me again when I ring," then he opened the letter and read as follows:

"I have spoken with Maud, dear Juan; and, I must admit, reproached her for the duplicity, which was even more reprehensible in her than in you. I have striven to do the best for you, though you would have served yourself better by confiding sooner in me. I find my niece is exceedingly anxious to feel herself quite free. She begs me to say she feels deeply the obligation under which she lies to you, and she hopes hereafter to reward your services ; but she would feel happier if you would send by bearer a *written* declaration that you hold the marriage ceremony you went through null and void. It pains me to write thus to you, for displeased, nay, agonised, as I have been, I think you deserve more confidence from *her*. But 'tis hard to change nature, and hers is somewhat cold. A declaration as above would also relieve me (if I have still any weight in your eyes) from some difficulty. John Langley claims the custody of his ward. While I could declare my ignorance of the gallant who kidnapped Harold Langley, and my desire to preserve Maud from him, I could with a safe conscience oppose those claims. I can scarce do so now unless by your renunciation.

"I have recommended, for obvious reasons, that Maud should keep her room, but should you wish to address her, enclose your billet to me and she shall receive it. She is, in truth, more composed than we could hope, but 'tis safer she should be reported *in-*disposed. Farewell, dear Juan, trust me I shall ever be your devoted friend, however small the guerdon of affection you accord to

"E. HELMSFORD."

Three times did Monteiro peruse this epistle before laying it down with some very strong Spanish expletives. He had a strong impression that it was written and composed without any knowledge on Maud's part. Maud had promised to trust him, and she would keep her word unless, indeed, Lady Helmsford had persuaded her to break it; even so Monteiro doubted that she had given her aunt permission to write thus, but to promise *him* reward for his services, as though he were an inferior, *that* she had never done! Lady Helmsford had out-witted herself there. If false in one point, why might not the letter be false in all?

He rang for Gomez and interrogated him. "Madam, her ladyship had been much at home and was not pleased with any one; had permitted Beville, that pig of a woman, to box him (Gomez) unrebuked. The beautiful Señorita he had not seen for days; many doctors had been to visit her, but she was still alive."

"Madre di Dios!" cried Monteiro, seizing him by the shoulders; "is she really ill? speak, little devil!"

"Grazia, Señor! I think she is not bad, for Madam Dorothy has been to and fro the housekeeper's room, and smiles, which she would not do were the Señorita ill."

"True, true," replied Monteiro, gazing away into vacancy, and still holding Gomez's shoulder.

"There is a preparation in the household, Excellency. They say the Countess leaves next week for Paris; Señor Chifferil left this morning."

"Chifferil! What, for Paris?" exclaimed Monteiro, much struck.

"I cannot tell whither he went, Excellency; but he started betimes and was sore vexed to go."

"There is mischief afoot!" thought Monteiro; "Chifferil was a sheet-anchor in that house. Hark ye, Gomez," he said aloud; "I must write a letter for you to take, and whenever you hear the name of Langley— listen. Moreover, should the Señorita be worse, come and tell me; and stay! here is a line for Mistress Dorothy." He hastily scribbled a few lines. "Don't let mortal see it save Mistress Dorothy—eat it—swallow it, rather than give it up to any one else!"

Gomez nodded energetically, and placed it carefully in a tiny inner pocket that opened behind his third button.

They thought they had managed it neatly, little dreaming that poor Dorothy was safe under lock and key.

"Now for my lady the Countess," said Monteiro, taking pen and paper; after a moment's thought he wrote:

"DEAR LADY HELMSFORD,

"I have your note, but think it unnecessary now to say more than this— I will call upon you to-morrow afternoon, when we can discuss the matters you allude to.

"Always your faithful servant,

"JUAN DI MONTEIRO."

A piece of civil evasion which infuriated the Countess, even while it set her counting the hours till the next afternoon.

The next morning rose clear, bright, sharp, as became the first week of March. Monteiro rose early, and started in good time for Chelsea. He chose the river as his highway; his course passed the old gateway, sole relic remaining of York House, and Westminster stairs, away past the low-lying flats on the Surrey side and the numerous barges, wherries and pleasure-boats which business and an unusually fine day had brought forth to ply upon the silent highway.

Much did Monteiro muse on the characteristics of English life, and longed for the hour when he might claim his birthright of nationality.

He was too much a man to be only a lover, though his love was strong and deep. Still, even in his most passionate moments, he knew that were love swept out his life, life itself, action, ambition, would not be annihilated; though dull and dreary without the sun of warm affection, light enough would be left to work and win.

Thus thinking he landed and approached Sir Stephen Compton's house, which looked upon the river; it was separated from the road by high railings and stood alone, a large garden and pleasure-ground stretching behind it.

CHAPTER IV.

THE great wrought-iron gates closed behind Monteiro with a clang as he passed through them and pulled a large bell, the handle of which hung by the door.

It was soon thrown open, and with a polite invitation to enter, the footman who opened the door led Monteiro across a handsome hall (from which a noble flight of stairs with gilt balusters led to the rooms above) to a library at the back of the house, where breakfast was laid.

Monteiro strolled to the window and looked out on a pleasant garden, with clipped yew

43—2

trees and a sundial. Within, the walls were adorned with a few good Dutch pictures. Indian cabinets, China ornaments, and well-filled bookshelves, made up a very pleasing interior. Some specimens of feather and bead work were not unfamiliar to the visitor's eye, who guessed they were mementoes of Sir Stephen's short but restorative sojourn in his American Government.

Monteiro, however, was not left long to study the aspect of the chamber. A door, different from that by which he had entered, opened, and a lady whom he at once recognised as Mistress Compton, Sir Stephen's eldest daughter, entered. She was a tall and somewhat stiff figure, considerably past her first youth; she wore a dress of dark green lutestring, a white sprigged muslin apron and fichu, or cross-over, trimmed with narrow edging, and her pale brown weak-looking hair, turned back over a small cushion, was covered with a cap and lappets of the same lace; she was slightly rouged, but coloured beneath it with evident pleasure when she saw Monteiro. She made the usual curtsy, however, before addressing him, and then, holding out her hand in a long black lace mitten, she exclaimed :

"Captain Monteiro ! I am truly pleased to see you again !"

He took and bowed over the hand she offered.

"My father will be here directly," she continued, "but he is not so early as is his usual habit; he has scarce yet recovered his wearisome journey from Hanover."

"And he is infinitely good to admit me so soon ! Permit me, madam, to express the pleasure I feel on seeing you in apparently so much better health than when I bade you adieu—now more than two years ago !"

Mistress Compton smiled a kindly though wavering smile. She was one of the women who, at forty or fifty, have not outlived girlish timidity; a sweet slight nature not rich enough to ripen into true maturity, too sound and pure to be soured by years and disappointment; she might lose the freshness of youth, but could never gain the force and dignity of experience. Nevertheless, she had,.

unconsciously to herself, been the stay of her somewhat selfish and dilettante father, and the real bond of union between him and his younger daughter, who resembled him; both loved and sacrificed her!

" I am, thanks be to God, in much better health, sir," she returned. " I think the heat and cold of America tried me much; then the sore terror and pressing danger, from which you so gallantly delivered us, preyed long upon my nerves."

" And how fares Mistress Phillis, your sister?"

" She has been married a year and more," replied Mistress Compton, ringing for the breakfast to be served. " Married to Master Leatham, of Leatham Court in Wiltshire. I have just returned from visiting her, during my father's absence with the King. She knew that I was to see you, and charged me to deliver her best compliments and regards, hoping you will visit her at her country-seat, in which desire her husband begged to join."

Before Monteiro could make any answer

the door again opened to admit the master of
the house.

Sir Stephen Compton, though scarce of
middle stature, and now a mere shadow of
his former self, had evidently been a very
handsome man, and gave himself the " beauty
airs " which are not exclusively practised by
the fair sex. He was wrapped in a flowered
silk *robe-de-chambre*, and wore elaborately-
braided slippers ; but his wig was duly curled,
and his cravatte tied with studied negligence.

" Ah, my dear young friend ! I rejoice to
have an opportunity at last of welcoming
you to my house. It has been a devilishly
unlucky *contretemps* that I should have been
away when you first came to England ; but
we must make up for lost time. How goes
it, my gallant Captain ?"

So saying, the gay Baronet shook hands
with his guest very cordially.

" I am charmed to see both yourself and
Mistress Compton look so well, and greatly
indebted for this prompt admission to your
presence."

" Zounds, sir !" cried the host, " if *you* had
not been prompt on that terrible occasion, our
captors would have made short work with us!
But sit down, Monteiro—sit down. I really
feel the ghost of an appetite flittering in my
interior ; 'tis too rare and precious a visitant.
not to be gratified at once."

They placed themselves at table, Sir Stephen
speaking only of common topics while the servants were in the room.

" What will you take, my dear sir ? hot
tea ?   No, I thought not.   There is some very
decent Bordeaux ; and let me recommend that
Rhenish wine ; 'tis not yet much known or
liked in England, but I think it has a rare
flavour."

" Hand the cutlets to Captain Monteiro,"
said the lady of the house.

" Have you no *pâté*, Anne ?" asked her
father.

" Yes, sir ; 'tis opposite Captain Monteiro.
Pray help yourself, sir."

At last, the ghost of Sir Stephen's appetite
being laid, and the edge of his guest's blunted,
the servants were dismissed, and Mistress.

Compton, on a hint from her father, apologised, curtsied, and withdrew.

" Come, now, Monteiro ! let us discuss our plans," said Sir Stephen, stirring his second cup of chocolate. " By the way, what do you wish to be called ?"

" After I have been recognised by the King,. my real name—Langley. And tell me, sir, how do you think I stand ?"

" Well, my friend, right well ! I have told His Majesty your wondrous tale. Now, there's. no man to whom a bit of romantic gossip is so welcome as your Sovereign, whose life is one of unavoidable routine ; and I flatter myself I have primed him well. Thrice have I re-counted the chapter of our gallant rescue— decks slippery with blood, my rifled treasure-chest, our slaughtered crew, my terrified faint-ing daughters cruelly lashed to the mast, to await the brutality of our captors ; my own hands bound with every indignity behind me,. in expectation of walking the plank ; the sud-den clearing of the fog in which we had been enveloped ; the appearance as by magic of your gallant schooner, the first and well-

directed shot that cut the mainbrace, the desperate exploit of boarding from your boats,
the hand-to-hand encounter, and our final
deliverance. Then his gracious Majesty was
charmed to know the secret history of the
pardon, before Sunderland or Craggs or any
of them. Oh! you stand very well; moreover, I think the King is disposed to take you
into his service—there will be fighting with
Spain before the year is out. Tell me, Monteiro, why do you not marry the young
heiress? You would make her a capital
husband, and a proper Lord of Langdale;
those peerages in the female line are a mistake."

"Ah, Sir Stephen! how do you know the
lady would consent?"

"Pooh, pooh! I do not think so meanly
of you, but that you would know how to win
her. But tell me, now that we can converse
vivâ voce, how did you get hold of the
pardon?"

"'Tis as curious a story as the rest," said
Monteiro, declining the Rhenish, and helping
himself to Bordeaux. "You must know that

there was a certain Irishman (who had fought
at Blenheim, in King Louis' famous Irish
Brigade) in my father's service. I believe my
father had known him in Ireland at the siege
of Limerick; and, after finding him in sore
distress, took him on board *El Veloz* more
from compassion than any other motive.
Well, when after I had lost my noble father
and captain, and decided to renounce the sea,
D'Arcy, the man of whom I speak, was among
the first I disbanded. He had some wish to
return to Ireland, I believe, and, at any rate,
made his way to London. You must remember, he was of our party the night my
father was so treacherously murdered. Well,
being one day in a tavern, somewhere in
Whitefriars, he heard a half-tipsy ragamuffin
of a fellow boast that he was going to make
John Langley's fortune and his own ; that he
could supply what would make a nobleman of
Langley, and much to the same effect. D'Arcy
pricked up his ears at the name, plied the man
with liquor and questions, but could only draw
from him that he was going to see Langley
that evening to clinch the business. Some

lucky wave of thought suggested to D'Arcy
that whatever it was that lent the owner importance in John Langley's eyes, 'twas probably a written document, and on his person;
so D'Arcy watched and followed him. In a
suitable place he overtook and felled him to
the ground, rifled his pockets, and, sewn between the lining and outside of his coat, found
the pardon. D'Arcy could but half understand it. However, the names of Langdale
and Langley made him see it was of value."

"What marvellous luck! What an admirable bravo!" ejaculated Sir Stephen.

"He did not like to confide the document
to any one, so he wrapped it in a parcel, sealing
and directing it to me. This he gave into
the care of another old follower of ours, the
owner of Lambs' coffee-house, near Holborn."

"I know it," said Sir Stephen. "Go on."

"He managed to send me a few lines,
stating that the pardon was found ; but I had
sailed for France, and the letter did not reach
me. He managed to write a second, which
he did more than a month after date. He then
started for Paris, hoping to find me. We

crossed on the way, but we finally met at Lambs'; since which time I have waited with what patience I could muster for the King's return and yours."

" A marvellous tale as ever I heard !" cried Sir Stephen; " and meantime poor Langdale's daughter is safe ?" I mean, that scheming rascal, John Langley, has not succeeded in wedding her to his son ?"

" No, sir ! Her marriage with an unknown stranger has not yet been dissolved."

" Ah, I had forgotten ! That, too, is be-yond the ordinary run of gossip. Have you any idea who the hero of that shrewd plot ' can be ?"

Monteiro hesitated a moment. Should he speak out the whole truth ? A nameless re-luctance held him back.

" I have an idea," he said ; " but it is not yet time to utter it."

" Indeed !" replied Sir Stephen, looking at him keenly. " As you will ; and is the young lady still with Lady Helmsford ?"

" Yes," said Monteiro, and paused. " I am about to ask a great, perhaps too great a favour; but I have a notion that my Lady Helmsford is scarce all she might be to her niece; that, till her own household is organised, she might be better elsewhere. She is singularly destitute of friends and relatives. Would your daughter, the gentle Mistress Compton, object to receive her for awhile?"

The proposition seemed to astonish Sir Stephen greatly, but not disagreeably. He was exactly the sort of man to enjoy appearing in the character of the genial, disinterested protector of prosperous people.

"My dear friend, if it were possible the young lady would prefer the shelter of my poor roof to the splendour of her noble aunt's stately mansion, I need scarcely assure you that my house, myself, and all belonging to me are most heartily at your and her service. So you and your fair cousin understand each other! Eh, my cunning gallant! I begin to smell a rat."

"In truth, sir," said Monteiro, smiling frankly, "since you have so kindly and freely granted my prayer, I do not think it loyal to keep my secret from you any longer. I·am he who played the unhappy bridegroom's part in the Langdale marriage !"

" The devil you were ! Why, Monteiro, you would beat Condé himself in stratagem and resource ! So the heiress is yours ? I am indeed pleased at this intelligence ; but why the *unhappy* bridegroom ?"

" Because the lady declines to be my wife ; in short, my dear friend, I particularly wish to set her free, so soon as she is safely made a ward of Chancery, and in your charge."

" Then is the Countess of Helmsford over-anxious to push your marriage with her niece ?"

" Far from it ; she urges other claims. But all I want is that my fair and noble cousin shall be left quite free."

" 'Fore God, your honour is over-scrupulous ! How do you know the lady will prove un-kind ?"

" Let us discuss this no more," said Monteiro, firmly. " You have kindly promised to receive her, if necessary ; we must leave the rest to arrange itself. Now tell me, when may I hope to see the King ?"

" There, I have done great things for you !
His Majesty proposes to give you a private
audience, immediately after he has received
Lord Sunderland, the day after to-morrow—
Thursday.   What say you to that ?   I am to
present you !   Have the pardon at hand, His
Majesty can then confirm it, and the guardian-
ship of the heiress can be transferred to the
Chancellor."

" Your goodness—your energetic goodness
overwhelms me !" cried Monteiro, his heart
beating, his cheek flushing at the idea that
the longed-for day of deliverance was at
hand.

" My dear sir," returned the Baronet, with
polite gratitude, " even so, the balance of obligation will not be adjusted.   I am still heavily
your debtor.   You had better join me at the
palace about noon, or half-past ; we must be
at hand to obey the summons to His Majesty's
presence."

"You may trust my punctuality," said
Monteiro with a smile ; "and you believe all
will go well ?"

"I feel tolerably secure," replied Sir Stephen

calmly. " What I most fear is John Langley getting scent of our proceedings. He is, from all I hear, a shrewd, bold fellow, and stands well with Berkeley and Craggs. Had he succeeded in wedding the heiress to his son, all would have been safe for him ; he has interest enough to have had the attainder reversed. Had he time he would manage to be still left guardian. Do you know, my friend, it would be a good plan to persuade the young orphan to be your wife *de facto*, before Langley can make any disturbance. You surely do not mean to let slip so fair a chance of fortune ?"

" I do," said Monteiro resolutely. " God forbid I took advantage of the sore strait to which my noble kinswoman was reduced ! Besides, I am no match for her in fortune."

" Come, come, Monteiro ! you like some dark-eyed Spanish beauty ! hence these scruples ?"

" No, Sir Stephen !" cried Monteiro warmly " there's no woman to compare with Maud Langley in my mind. If I loved her less, I would have fewer scruples ; but she does not care to admit my claims. She is so young, so

tender, and has been so sorely tried, she has
no thought for love."

"She must be a very remarkable young
woman," said Sir Stephen dryly. "However,
a true lover is, they say, modest, though 'tis
not exactly the quality I should expect in a
bold buccaneer. You know your own affairs
best, no doubt. At all events, the young
lady will be an honoured and a favoured guest
in my house."

After some more discussion and settlement
of the details of Monteiro's presentation, they
adjourned to Mistress Compton's morning-
room, where they found her copying some
letters for her father. Sir Stephen explained
the intended interview with the King, and its
object, giving a short graphic account of Maud
Langley's position, suppressing, however, the
mysterious marriage with her cousin.

The kind Mistress Compton was deeply
interested, and warmly assured Monteiro of
the pleasure it would give her to welcome his
kinswoman, but appeared to share her father's
surprise at his wish to remove her from the
care of her aunt.

Then Sir Stephen insisted on showing his pictures and objects of " vertu " to Monteiro, talking a jargon concerning them which was Greek to his hearer, whose patience was sorely tried. He burned to be alone, to arrange his thoughts, to marshal his mental forces, and strengthen himself for the act of renunciation he feared was before him. He would be stronger, he thought, but for the memory of Maud's accent when she uttered the last words he had heard from her lips— " May God protect you!" To this remembered music he listened with all his soul, while Sir Stephen prated of foregrounds and " chiaroscuro," " flesh tints," and " depth of colour," the accomplished Baronet thinking all the time how graceful and admirable was his *protégé's* gravity and attention.

At last Sir Stephen's coach was announced, and Monteiro was released. " Let me set you down at your lodgings ; I believe you have no conveyance waiting," said the courteous host ; and Monteiro accepted.

But on the road he changed his destination. He could not resist the eager desire to ascer-

tain how matters were going on at St. James's
Square.   Perhaps Lady Helmsford might be
out ; in any case he would see Maud.   So he
stopped the carriage in Pall Mall, bade Sir
Stephen good-day, and proceeded to Lady
Helmsford's house, his heart beating high, his
veins thrilling with the hope that the weary
time of prudence, waiting, and inaction was
at last over, or nearly over.   It was the omis-
sion from his thoughts of that little qualifying
word "nearly," implying "not completely,"
which threw Monteiro off his guard.

The time which had elapsed since the Countess had imprisoned Maud in her chamber was
the most miserable of her life.   Mortified and
disappointed beyond the power of language to
convey, Lady Helmsford found it impossible,
even with her trained social skill, to face
society with becoming composure.   She kept
the house—her own private apartments—
reckless of what society might say.   She
ordered Beville to reply to inquiries by stating
that she was occupied with Mistress Langley,
who was seriously unwell, and with prepara-

tions for her journey to Paris, whither she
intended to remove her niece. Really, her
plans were chaotic. She did intend to leave
London ; but, respecting Maud, she changed
from hour to hour. She felt how cruel it
would be to abandon her to John Langley ;
she knew how ill it would look for herself.
Moreover, it would be an unsatisfactory revenge, and one which would convert Monteiro
from a possible lover into a bitter hater ; besides, she was not without some feeling for
Maud, though desperately enraged by her
spirit and innate dignity. She had not seen
her since she had ordered her to her room ;
she shrank from the idea of meeting her eyes.
At times she thought of her youth, her
isolation, her helplessness. Again the vision
of Juan suing to her with all the tenderness
and passion she felt, rather than knew, he
could express, set her blood on fire with rage
and hatred. He had been guarded in his
speech respecting Maud, but the tone of his
voice, the expression of his face, revealed
more than she dared to recall. And he was
Maud Langley's husband ! A word, a look

from her might convert the marriage into a reality. For Lady Helmsford knew enough of the daring and resolution of her former admirer, to feel sure that he only wanted his bride's consent to dare, and evade all that guardian and protectress could do to keep her from him.

Tossed thus on the tempestuous sea of her own thoughts, Lady Helmsford's sole comfort was derived from the prospect of leaving London. A vague unreasonable hope tinged her dreary horizon—the hope that once she was really gone, Monteiro would follow. But what—what should she do with Maud? She hurried on the preparations for her journey with feverish energy, and gave strictest orders that Mistrsss Maud and her woman should have everything they desired, save liberty; she even sent a kind message to her niece, assuring her that it was best and safest for her to be imprisoned, and then wished she could recall it.

The same morning that Monteiro breakfasted with Sir Stephen Compton, Lady Helmsford was roused from her deep, sullen abstraction, as she brooded moodily over her dressing-room fire, by the entrance of Beville, who said :

" Master John Langley is below, and begs to be admitted to your ladyship."

" Admit him," returned the Countess, without an instant's hesitation.

" How, my lady ! here ?" Beville was a little uneasy at her mistress's strange ways of . late.

" Well, in the next room."

" And your dress, my lady ?"

" 'Tis good enough for the fellow ; do not be an idiot, Beville—bring him up."

Beville, much wondering, obeyed.

" Well, Master Langley," cried the Countess, walking into the study which adjoined her dressing-room, " I have expected to see you."

" Indeed, madam !" returned Langley, looking with some surprise at the unusual negligence of her dress. " I have called in consequence of a rumour that has reached me. Is it true that your ladyship means to leave for Paris immediately ?"

"I do not know," she returned, gazing as if she saw him not.

"Surely your ladyship must know your own intentions ?"

"Scarce exactly," she replied, collecting herself.

"Because I must resume the custody of my ward's person, if such is the case," said Langley. "I have from courtesy postponed intruding my physician upon Mistress Langley, but I can do so no longer ; he now awaits your permission to ascend and ascertain her present condition."

" 'Tis needless," said Lady Helmsford slowly, and motioning Langley to a seat. "My niece is well—well enough to go to your house, to travel, to do anything."

"Your ladyship is frank," said Langley, surprised and fearing a trap. "I rejoice to receive so good a report of Mistress Langley's health. I presume then, that to-morrow at furthest she may take up her abode in my house ?"

Lady Helmsford was silent for a moment, and then said, looking very straight into John

Langley's eyes, "You are, of course, at liberty
to take her to-morrow; but I ask you to
wait. I may wish to *send* her to you to-
morrow; I may wish to keep her with me
till I go to Paris. Will you leave it thus,
Master Langley? You may trust me; I no
longer wish to assume the task of protecting
Maud Langley. She is wilful and troublesome! Do you still think of wedding her to
your son?"

"I see no reason to alter my intentions,"
returned Langley, conscious of a perceptible
though subtle change in the Countess, who
spoke and moved like one in a sort of dream,
or acting mechanically under some strong
pressure. But I will leave the task of recon-
ciling her to my son. I—ahem—" for an
instant the enormous lie troubled Langley's
utterance—" I was not aware the young man
was so partial to his cousin; and probably
when she sees him worn by sickness—sickness caused by her cruelty—her feelings may
alter."

" Perhaps so—perhaps so," said the Countess very thoughtfully, while her heart

whispered, "it is possible! girls are weak and easily persuaded; but if she can be induced to wed Harold, Monteiro is mine! How is your son, sir?" she added aloud.

"Better, madam, though still weak. I have sent him to the country, for change of air and quiet."

"That's well. But how about his arm, Master Langley? They say it was broken."

"They say—who says?" asked Langley angrily. "Does your ladyship believe all the gossip that idlers invent?"

"I am glad 'tis not so," returned Lady Helmsford carelessly. She was growing anxious to dismiss him; she did not feel equal to the task of fencing. Her consciousness of the cruelty she knew she would be guilty of, weakened and confused her. As George Eliot writes, "The concentrated experience which, in great crises of emotion, reveals the bias of a nature, is prophetic of the ultimate act, which will end an intermediate struggle." As yet she shrank from the baseness of delivering the young helpless orphan, who had trusted her, into the hands of so implacable a foe as her guardian—to a fate she dreaded worse than death—but in her inmost soul she knew she would do it. "If the young gentleman," she resumed after a moment's pause, "is so much attached to my niece, I can but wish him success. I am not yet too old, Master Langley," she added with a smile, which even John Langley felt was charming, "to sympathise with true love."

Langley was greatly puzzled. Something in her tone and manner conveyed a certain conviction of her sincerity; and yet he could not, and would not trust her. The utmost he would permit himself to believe was that some whim, some unexpressed cause of offence against her niece, had operated on Lady Helmsford to his (Langley's) advantage, and he must, if possible, seize the auspicious moment.

"Then, madam, why should we lose time? If your ladyship is thus well disposed towards my boy, permit me to resume the guardianship of my ward to-day, or at furthest to-morrow?"

"To-day!" cried the Countess in an accent
of pain; "no, not to-day! no, not to-day!
Why are you in such haste? you mean no ill
to my sister's daughter! no, I am sure you
do not! if you did—look you, Master Langley,
with all your legal rights you should not have
her! If I, Elizabeth of Helmsford, resolved,
really resolved to keep her, it would be strange
if I did not!"

"Probably, madam," replied Langley,
shrewd enough to see that there was some
motive working in her heart which would
serve his cause better than contradiction.
"I believe we are both anxious to befriend
this peevish young woman; for the present
I leave her in your hands, and while promising to leave her free in the matter of her
marriage, I also confide my son's cause to
your honour; if you will not help his suit, at
least do nought to prejudice it!"

"I promise," said the Countess, rising;
"let my niece stay with me a few days more,
I may not leave for Paris quite so soon; at
any rate you shall have due warning."

"I shall do myself the honour of calling

to-morrow," replied Langley, also rising, and accepting the dismissal with a bow.

"What! do you mistrust me, sir?" cried Lady Helmsford.

"Far be it from me to distrust your ladyship," he returned dryly. "But as we have now joined forces 'tis but natural I should be in communication with my ally."

The blood mounted to Lady Helmsford's cheek, but she restrained the words that rose to her lips.

"I will bid you good-day, sir," she said coldly; "I am somewhat indisposed."

"Adieu, then, madam; I leave your ladyship with the clear understanding that you admit my full rights as guardian of your niece, and are prepared to yield them when the time for your departure arrives."

"I wish you good-day, sir," repeated the Countess, curtsying, so Langley had nothing for it but to bow himself out.

"Her fate is in her own hands," murmured Lady Helmsford, still standing where he had left her. "If she will but be guided by me —what is John Langley, his hopes, his

schemes, compared to my regard for Monteiro?
—I will be Maud's friend, and a true, powerful friend, *if* she will let me, but 'tis in her
own hands!" She turned from the table by
which she stood and walked slowly into her
dressing-room. "Beville," she said to that
functionary, who was sorting and arranging a
drawer full of lace; "how fares Mistress
Langley? have you spoken with her this
morning?"

"No, my lady; Cicely took in breakfast
when she went to make up the bed-chamber."

"How is this!" cried Lady Helmsford
indignantly; "do you dare neglect my niece
and leave her to be attended by a mere
serving-wench? though for her safety sake I
am obliged to keep her under lock and key,
think you I would have her treated with
scant respect?"

"I know your ladyship is all goodness,"
replied Beville, pursing up her mouth; "but
if you only just heard how that unmannerly
female, Mistress Dorothy Keen, abuses me,
you would not wonder at my avoiding her!
There is nothing too bad, and too aggravating

for her to say, and she even hints at *you*, my lady !"

" 'Tis of small consequence," said the Countess carelessly ; " the woman is faithful, she does not understand my motives, and you must not therefore neglect her mistress."

" I suppose, my lady, that villain wants to run away with her again !" insinuated Mistress Beville, who, as well as Mistress Letitia Sparrow, had been much exercised in her mind respecting the strange action of the Countess in imprisoning her niece.

" He does !" she replied, clenching her teeth as if in pain ; " and he shall not have her !"

" Mistress Langley desired to have speech with your ladyship," resumed Beville.

" I cannot see her to-day—I cannot !" cried Lady Helmsford. " Stay, Beville ; take her a little note, or perhaps they would like Sparrow to go instead of you ?"

" Oh ! as your ladyship pleases !" returned Beville, with a toss of the head ; " only Mistress Sparrow is so fond of my young lady, she will be leaving the lock unturned or some such trick, for that woman Dorothy

craves so to be let roam about the house,
that I'd wager the pair of lovely lace ruffles
your ladyship gave me, against Molly the
kitchen-maid's linen kerchief, that she has
some scheme for getting her mistress free!"

" 'Tis not so unlikely," said Lady Helmsford.

"And then," continued the waiting-woman,
seeing she had produced an impression, "if
your ladyship would not be angry, I caught
that little——black fellow," Beville just
suppressed an unflattering epithet in time,
"twice lingering about the door and peeping
through the key-hole."

"Did you?" cried the Countess, roused to
instant maddening perception. "He! Monteiro's gift! I must look to this!"

She stopped in deep thought; the possibility of communications between Monteiro
and Maud through her little black favourite
flashed through her brain with a sudden
sickening sense of treachery, of being opposed
by a will as strong and tenacious as her own,
of failure and defeat. What! Gomez as well
as Chifferil wavering in their allegiance to

her ? both interwoven by Monteiro into the
subtle web of watchfulness, with which he
managed to surround that insignificant child
by whom his thoughts seemed to be absorbed !

" Ah !" exclaimed Lady Helmsford at last,
" bring my writing things !" she quickly
traced a few lines. " There !" she said folding
and directing it, " tell Giles, the head groom,
to take this note to Mistress Ferrars, and let
him take Gomez too ; let him see Gomez into
the house, and then return, the little fellow
is better suited to deliver a note to a lady
than Giles. Stay," seeing a curious gleam in
her waiting-maid's eyes, " light a taper, I
will seal the billet ! There, Beville, see them
off ; tell Giles not to lose sight of him."

This despatched, she wrote a few civil
words for her niece, which were ready for
transmission when Beville returned ; then she
lay back in her chair and thought—sometimes
with painful clearness, sometimes with aching
indistinctness, but always unpleasantly and
with a tinge of despair—of the terrible
collapse of all her hopes, of the straws to

which she clung, of the dust and ashes into which her life had crumbled. Now, for the first time in her prosperous existence, she was struggling with a real sorrow; she lived over and over again her brief acquaintance with Monteiro in Paris, accusing and excusing him as contending waves of feeling swept over her storm-driven soul.

CHAPTER V.

INUTES or hours, Lady Helmsford knew not which, had passed thus when Beville again intruded herself.

"Don Monteiro is below," she said, eying the Countess sharply as she spoke, "and begs to speak with your ladyship."

"Monteiro!" cried Lady Helmsford, starting from the large chair in which she had been reclining. "Yes, of course!—No, I cannot, Beville; my *déshabille* is too outrageous: tell him I am unwell—suffering; if he really wishes to see me he may return in an hour. Come back directly with his reply—quickly, Beville."

45—2

The Countess remained in the same position, grasping the arm of her chair, as if turned to stone, during the short absence of her attendant.

"Don Monteiro will await your ladyship's pleasure," was the reply brought back by the envoy.

"Quick, then, Beville! I will only adopt a *négligée*, and the faintest tinge of rouge! or none?"

Lady Helmsford started to life as Beville spoke, and rushed to her toilette-table with these words: "How say you, Beville," looking intently into her glass, "rouge or none?"

"La! my lady, you look like a ghost."

"And men are seldom touched by ghostly looks, however deep the suffering they express! but Juan has feeling! I would fain stir his compassion. Now, Beville; how dull and slow you are! Give me my morning robe of crimson taffetas and velvet, roll up my hair! loosely, woman, loosely; if I discard the array of a full toilette at least let me show the wealth of nature! What said Monteiro to you?"

" He asked keenly for Mistress Langley, my lady," replied the waiting-woman in return for her mistress's abrupt imperiousness.

" Ha ! well, Chifferil and Gomez are out of the way ; none else will dare prate to him of the discipline I am forced to use : but "— with a sudden eager flash of her dark eyes— " where is that fantastic ape, Sparrow ? Go ! call her this instant, Beville — go !" and Lady Helmsford stamped her foot with impatience.

Mistress Beville, nothing loath, hurried away, and fetched the amiable Letitia from an elaborate task of millinery which she was performing in the congenial society of Mab and Tab.

The *dame de compagnie* looked not a little startled and uneasy as she followed Beville into the room.

" Where did you find her ?" cried the Countess abruptly.

" Above stairs, in her own room, my lady," returned Beville.

" That is well ! Tell me, Sparrow, have you been to see my niece this morning ?"

" No, my lady."

" Nor yesterday ?"

" No, my lady; in truth, Mistress Beville seemed that fractious about my visiting Mistress Langley that——"

"Quite right, Sparrow—quite right," interrupted Lady Helmsford ; "to-morrow you can see her—to-morrow all may be well; we will prepare for our journey to Paris : you must believe, Sparrow, that I am in all things ruled by an ardent desire to serve my niece—though after all, why should I care a straw what you think ?"

" Indeed, my lady, I am sure your solicitude——"

" There, there ! do not prate to me—I want nothing more. But stay—stay where you are !" for Letitia had moved with alacrity to the door at this apparent dismissal—"stay till I have finished dressing."

This undertaking was now quickly completed, and Beville directed to summon Don Juan di Monteiro.

" Here," exclaimed the Countess, " here are some new ribbons for Mab and Tab ; go, my good Sparrow, and adorn those little creatures, and remain with them, in readiness should I require you to bring them to me."

Having thus secured all approaches to her secret, Lady Helmsford swept into the adjoining room, and, for a few suffocating seconds, awaited the coming of her lost lover. And when he came his face, his very form, seemed penetrated by a new life; there was a brilliancy, a depth of colour in his eyes, and elasticity in his step that bespoke joy and triumph. But when his glance fell on the Countess his expression changed and softened. She looked indeed ill and worn, though her eyes were feverishly bright, and nothing affected the grace of her superb figure.

" Dios !" he cried ; " it is indeed true ! you have been ill, dear lady ? how goes it with you now ?"

" Do not ask me, Juan ! I *have* been suffering—more in mind than body ; but let me rest ! what brings you here ? what and whom do you seek ?"

" You, in the first place," he returned, leading her by the hand she had given him to

a seat; "I want to report progress to you,
and then—then I want to see Maud—Mistress
Langley I mean. I have good news, fair
Countess ; the King will see me on Thursday.
In forty-eight hours I hope to see your niece
proclaimed Baroness Langdale : may I not see
her in your presence ?

"You cannot," replied Lady Helmsford,
pressing her hand to her brow, so as to hide
her face for a moment, while she struggled to
control its expression. "She too is unwell,
or captious ; she will not see me ; she has
locked herself in her own room, and insists on
being undisturbed."

"Then she has either been offended or
alarmed !" exclaimed Monteiro. "Tell me,
dear Lady Helmsford ! do tell me the whole
truth !—is she really ill ? She has had so
much to try her, I tremble to think how her
spirits must be shaken : I am sure she will
see me ! I need not trouble her to descend
—I might go to her : ask her, sweet Countess.
Say I have tidings of importance ! she will
not refuse !"

The eager anxiety of his voice and manner

struck a deadly chill to his hearer's heart—
no words could have shown her so clearly
how his whole being was devoted to her
rival.

"What!" she cried, shrinking as if from a
blow, "do you already seek to husband's
privileges? Would you visit your bride in her
chamber?

"Hush, madam!" returned Monteiro sternly,
while the dark red flush of anger rose to his
cheek; "you well know how far such a hope is
from my thoughts! It is not for you—her
protectress—to suggest it."

"So much the better," said Lady Helmsford coldly; "for you do not seem very
acceptable to the young lady. I have had a
long conversation with her—which I am not
at liberty to repeat—touching her life in
France; and am bound to say I approve her
motives for wishing to dissolve the singular
tie which exists between you."

"Ah! then my fears——" began Monteiro
impetuously, while the colour faded from his
face; but something in Lady Helmsford's
eyes made him check his words. "Her dis-

regard of me," he resumed firmly, "has nothing to do with the service to which I have devoted myself. I still demand to see Mistress Langley in your presence; do you wish to prevent our meeting?"

"You shall see," replied Lady Helmsford, rising and going into the next room. She was scarce a whole minute absent: "Beville is not there!" she said; "ring yourself, Don Juan di Monteiro, and I will send your message to your wife."

"Do not mock me with this cruel repetition of a name I dare not, even in my heart, apply to the noble lady I only ask to serve," cried Monteiro passionately, but not forgetting to ring the bell indicated to him, and that with some vehemence. "You seem certain she would never admit my claim, even if I advanced it! Why then insult me thus? Is it from a simple love of giving pain?"

"Pain—to you! Ah, Heaven!" exclaimed Lady Helmsford, great tears filling her eyes and welling over unnoticed. "*You* know best how much I would endure and renounce to give you pleasure!"

"So it would seem," said Monteiro harshly.

The entrance of a footman prevented any reply.

"Where is Beville? send her to me!" exclaimed the Countess.

The man retired.

"Where is Mistress Sparrow?" asked Monteiro, with dim uneasiness.

"How can I tell? do you wish to pick and choose amid *my* household?" returned the Countess haughtily.

Monteiro bowed in silence.

Beville lost no time in presenting herself.

"Go to Mistress Langley," said Lady Helmsford, very slowly and distinctly; "tell her that Don Juan di Monteiro is here, and has matters of importance to communicate, and that I also desire her presence; if she is averse to leave her own apartments we will visit her there."

Beville curtsied, and went on her errand. During her absence an awkward and constrained silence fell upon the Countess and her companion : the former sat resting her

arm on the table beside her, leaning her head
on her hand—Monteiro standing by the fireplace, still and stern, his eyes fixed on the
door by which he expected Mistress Beville
to re-enter.

"Mistress Langley's duty to your ladyship ;
she does not wish to see Don Monteiro, or
any one. She is indisposed, and begs the
gentleman to send his message," said Beville
on her return.

"That will do—you may go," said Lady
Helmsford ; "unless indeed you wish to *send*
your message," turning to Monteiro, and
speaking with a slight tinge of scorn.

"That I shall not," he replied quickly,
irritated by a vague suspicion of foul play,
yet afraid of making a mistake by attacking
the Countess. "If Mistress Langley is unwell, it is not for me to intrude upon her ; if
she has no desire to learn my tidings from
myself, I need be in no haste to announce
them."

Beville disappeared. A short silence ensued : Monteiro walked to the window and
back, then threw himself into a chair.

"Come, Lady Helmsford," he exclaimed, "we have ever been good friends—tell me truth, however bitter! Why has Maud— why has your niece turned against me? What have you said of me? What has she confided to you? Is she—does she think of any one before me?—some lover in France— some—oh! speak! do not look at me as if you knew all and would say nothing."

Stretching out his hand, he seized hers, and grasped it painfully tight; but the Countess bore the pressure without flinching. Monteiro, in his passion, was forgetting that he had, to a certain length, played the part of this woman's lover : he felt so sure of Maud's freedom in another day, that he was off his guard.

Lady Helmsford pressed his hand for an instant, and then with a sudden impulse of impatience flung it from her.

"How dare I tell the truth to one so infatuated as you are!" she exclaimed with sudden vehemence. "Even were I not pledged to guard Maud's confidence, I dare not speak it."

"Break no pledge for me, madam," said Monteiro scornfully. "I see that whatever your motive, you do not intend to tell me truth."

"Yes I will, Juan," cried the Countess. "You are flattering yourself with false hopes. Maud does *not* love you ; she is barely grateful to you ; she shrinks from you ; her cold, thin, passionless nature is revolted by the fervour of yours. You waste your wealth of love on one who would be satisfied with coin less rich. Oh ! how is it that you turn from a heart as glowing as your own ! for one so poor, so weak, so irresponsive !"

In the agony of her supplication, Lady Helmsford stretched out her arms to Monteiro, her lips quivering, her dark eyes brimming over with unregarded tears. But Monteiro was inexorable. Irritated by a consciousness of treachery he must not express, made savage by this attack upon Maud, and the tone in which it was uttered, by a woman he did not think worthy to dust her shoes, he burst forth relentlessly :

"Irresponsive to me if you will," he exclaimed, springing to his feet and standing opposite the wretched suppliant, "but neither poor nor weak. If the purity and inexperience of her undeveloped nature make her shrink from the abruptness of my attempt to woo her, the fault is mine! There is the virgin gold of affection, the truest flames of love, under the snow of her present indifference, for him who shall be so blest as to call them forth! This may not be my lot; but shall I therefore be less ardent in her service? I am no foolish boy to fancy my mood will never change. I hope it will, if it brings me nothing save sorrow; but I tell you I would dare everything, forego everything, to feel the willing clasp of Maud Langley's arms— the touch of her cheek against mine—to hear her call me husband!"

He paused, breathless with his own vehemence.

Lady Helmsford had slowly dropped her arms as he spoke, the light and moisture leaving her eyes, and the colour fading even from her lips. She stood fixed and silent, her face hardening into a deadly expression.

"This may never be," resumed Monteiro, regardless of the woman he was torturing; "but no insinuations, however cunningly masked, will ever persuade me that Maud cares more for any other man than for myself. I understand her better than you do, madam. Love enlightens more than hatred."

He paused again. It was a bitter, almost a brutal, speech to one who, whatever her faults, he knew loved him well. But though Monteiro had perhaps more than the ordinary share of chivalrous feeling, he was not so far removed from other men that he could restrain the relentless cruelty which is almost invariably called forth by women who grovel at their feet even while they cross their wills. Upstanding, ay! and at her full height, is the only attitude in which woman can successfully deal with her master.

There was something ominous in the dead silence which followed, in the unwavering firmness of Lady Helmsford's pose.

"I understand the full meaning of your words, Monteiro," she said at last, slowly, as if giving heed to what she said. "I under-

stand the insulting comparison, between myself and my niece, which they convey. You
have perhaps cut out the roots of my disorder a trifle ruthlessly. It only remains for
me to give the surgeon his fee. Do you
doubt that I shall pay in full ?"

" I have no time or inclination to read
riddles. If your ladyship has no further
commands, I will wish you good-morning."

" Not yet," said the Countess impressively.
" Not yet, Monteiro—listen. How is it that
you who know *me*—you who know to the full
the dangers which threaten the woman who is
now the object of your passion, against which
I am now her sole protection—how dare you
exasperate me ! You must surely credit me
with more generosity then that of women ! I
might take a terrible revenge ! Bold and
resolute, and inventive as you are, you are a
stranger—single-handed—almost unknown—
what are you against the weight and
authority of English law ? A word from me,
and Maud——"

" You dare not," interrupted Monteiro,
startled but not frightened ; " you dare

not call in John Langley to aid your revenge! I am not single-handed now; forty-
eight hours will give me rights which will
supersede his. And for yourself, madam,
think how such a tale, circulating like a snow-
ball, with additions at every turn, will em-
blazon your name and character."

"I thank you for the friendly counsel," said
Lady Helmsford, with a grand curtsy. "But
do you not perceive that you have dragged
me through the depths of degradation to the
pinnacle of indifference !" Then with a sudden
change of tone, "Never again can tongues
wound me. Beware, Monteiro ! you shall not
insult and brave me with impunity."

Something in her voice made him feel he
had been incautious, and renewed his anger
with her by showing him his error.

"By Heavens !" he cried, "I shall force my
way to Maud's apartments, and carry her
away in the teeth of your household, rather
than let her suffer even the temporary terror
of your temper. I have found a safe and
honourable asylum for her." He made a quick
movement towards the door as he spoke.

" Do so !" cried Lady Helmsford, throwing
herself between him and it. " Do so. Force
yourself on her privacy, with this mere suspicion of yours as an excuse, and ruin your
chances. Hear me, Monteiro! in justice,
hear me !"

The Countess in her turn began to see that
premature threats hinder their own fulfilment. The earnestness of her tone, the pro-
bability of her words made Monteiro pause.

" You do not indeed know me yet," she
went on quickly, pressing one hand under her
bosom as she spoke. " You have cruelly
wronged and goaded me ! Now compare my
actions with my words. Scarce two hours
ago John Langley stood where you do. He
demanded Maud to be given into his hands
this day. I changed my tactics. For your
sake—ay—and for that of the—" Lady
Helmsford stopped an instant, and added in
a curiously softened tone, half whispered—
" the gentle girl herself. I stooped to speak
flatteringly to the fellow. I persuaded him to
grant me a little longer time ; talked of my
journey to Paris (I am really going, Juan, so

soon as Maud's affairs are settled), and so he
yielded and left, thinking he understood me.
He will not trouble me again till I announce
my intended departure. This will give you
time, will it not?"

Again Monteiro's brown cheek flushed,
quite as much for the doubts that still lingered
in his heart, as for shame at the possible in-
justice he had done.

"Madam! this is indeed a noble revenge
for my hasty words; but will you in truth
and honour still keep my secret, and hold to
the compact you have made with John
Langley?"

The Countess smiled. "I see you still
distrust me. On my word I solemnly promise that I will retract nothing I have
arranged with John Langley. In return, I
ask that you do not come here to disturb me
till after your interview with the King, then,
if all goes well, I will hand over the custody
of my niece to the safe and honourable
guardianship you say you have found for her.
You may trust me, Juan."

"I will—I do!" cried Monteiro, casting

away his doubts. "You are your own noble self again, and I will trust you utterly. Hereafter I may be able to prove my penitence and gratitude. I will trespass no longer upon you. Suffer me to kiss your hand ere I leave."

"No," said Lady Helmsford, stepping back quickly ; "not now. On Thursday, when you have seen the King, and return triumphant to show Maud your great services, you shall kiss it, if you will."

She smiled one of her proud sweet smiles, which all the world thought so charming.

"You forgive my irritation and unreasonableness ?"

"We shall exchange forgiveness, *mon ami*, on Thursday."

"Farewell, then, madam," said Monteiro, and retired, his last look at Lady Helmsford remaining long imprinted on his memory, as she stood motionless, one hand resting on the back of a chair, the other clenched, and lying at the full stretch of her arm against her dress—the sweep of her robe, her very smile and the turn of her head seemingly fixed as if carved in marble.

" She is a fine creature, and I am a brute to doubt her. After all, I said nothing so *very* offensive, that I can remember ; but my lady was always touchy."

So thinking, his heart full of Maud and doubts if she would ever consent to be his, Monteiro made his way to his lodgings, his fears for the time laid to rest.

Lady Helmsford stood for some time in the same position as when Monteiro left; then she made a sudden staggering movement forward, as if she would have fallen, but, clutching the back of the chair, she saved herself. With a strong effort she mastered her feelings, and walked into her dressing-room, where she plentifully bathed her head and face with cold water, and even after this unwonted operation sat and thought intensely, before she rang for Beville.

When that personage made her appearance she was startled by her lady's wild and haggard look.

"La! my lady, you are, sure, not well! What ails your ladyship?"

"Nothing, Beville; nothing you can help me in; yet you can! I want to go forth to-night with the strictest secrecy. You must lend me your cloak and hood and petticoat. Bring them at once. I must see Mistress Sparrow. I shall tell her I am ill, that she must watch in the outer room, and let none come near me, as you are going out. Then, Beville, we will lock the door. You shall stay in my place, and I will go in yours. Bespeak a chair to take you—oh! somewhere; you surely have cronies whom you visit? On my return I will tap at the farther door of my room. You can let me in, and we will change places again. Oh, Beville, be true to me now, and I will make your fortune!"

"That I will, my lady," said the waiting-woman heartily.

A day and night and part of another day had elapsed since Maud's imprisonment, and still she had received no communication from her aunt; nor had her messages been noticed.

It was a period of great trial and uneasiness. What were the Countess's intentions in her present exasperated mood? At times, with a vivid recollection of Lady Helmsford's angry looks of hatred, Maud feared the worst, and *her* worst meant being abandoned to the mercy of John Langley. At these moments she regretted not having yielded to Monteiro's prayer, and even risked being his wife, rather than the horrors that awaited her were she given back to her guardian. Monteiro, or Rupert as she called him to herself, would surely have been kind and tender—perhaps he was the only true friend she had in the wide world; yet she blushed and trembled, even to shrinking, at the idea of giving herself to so great a stranger. Indeed she wondered that he was ready to link himself to one he knew so little, for her ideas of love and marriage were very sober and delicate; yet, the notion of his possible preference for the Countess gave her a keen and deadly pain.

Then again, instance after instance of her aunt's generosity and pride came to her mind, and she rejected with indignation against her-

self the idea of treachery being possible to so
naturally noble a character. Yet she was
very wroth at being thus a prisoner for no
error deserving punishment. She felt she
could never again seek her aunt's friendship
or offer her her own. It was an insult as
well as an injury that could not soon be for-
given. As to Dorothy, no words could ade-
quately express her indignation and terror.
Her faith in Lady Helmsford's generosity and
loyalty was considerably more limited than
Maud's; but her anxiety to spare her beloved
young lady as much as possible kept her
unusually silent.

"Well, here is supper at last!" she exclaimed the evening of the day on which
Lady Helmsford had the stormy interview
above described with Monteiro. "It is not
that I am so hungry as that it's something to
do! Come, dear lamb! come to table, for we
know not how soon it may please my lady to
starve us; and I suppose Cicely there would
come in just as bright and smiling to say,
'Please, madam, you are to have no more to
eat,' as she does now to say, 'Please, madam,

I have brought supper,'" grumbled Dorothy as she assisted to lay the cloth.

"That would I not, Mistress Dorothy," said the young girl earnestly. "I am main sorry to have to turn the key on my lady here. But what can I do? Mistress Beville says 'tis all for her good, and shall not last long."

"Ah! indeed, Cicely, you are a good creature," quoth Dorothy. "Now, what's to prevent you letting me have a bit of a turn just for the good of my health?"

In truth, poor Dorothy was feverishly anxious to communicate with Monteiro, in whom, as by instinct, she put her trust as being able and willing to deliver her mistress.

"I can't, indeed I can't!" exclaimed Cicely, almost in tears. "Mistress Beville sits atop of the first flight of stairs, waiting for the key, and I dare not let you out."

"The devil fly away with Mistress Beville!" ejaculated Dorothy. "Ah! what are we shut up for at all? Anyhow, Cicely, tell us the news."

, " Indeed, Mistress Dorothy, there is none.
The house is like the dead! My lady is not
well. No visitors are let in—so Master
Hobson says ; and Mistress Beville desired me
to tell you, you are to pack up Mistress Maud's
mails, for my lady talks of starting for France
the day after to-morrow !"

" Indeed !" cried Maud, joining the conversation for the first time. " This is somewhat
unexpected !"

" No, madam ; preparations have been made
for the last few days."

" Tell me," asked Maud, much distressed
by this intelligence, "do you know if the
King has arrived ?"

" He hath, madam! He arrived the day
before yesterday, I believe. Did you not hear
the bells a-ringing ?"

" 'Tis strange no word has been sent me.
Stay, good Cicely ! It will not bring you
into mischief to take a note from me to my
aunt ?"

" Surely not, sweet lady ! Any ways I will
do your bidding."

Maud wrote a few lines, urgently im-

ploring to see and speak with Lady Helmsford ; and Cicely readily took charge of
them.

When she returned to remove their supper
things however, she only brought a verbal
message that the Countess would reply presently.

"It is all oppressively strange," said Maud
when she was once more alone with Dorothy.
"Why should my aunt hurry me away just
when the King returns ?　Why does not
M. di Monteiro make no sign ?　I seem suddenly cut off from help at the very crisis of
my fate."

"And I shut up like a malefactor, or I'd
soon know the whys and wherefores !" cried
Dorothy, wringing her hands distractedly.
"I'll go bail Master Monteiro has been here,
and not let come near ye !　Ah ! what has
happened to my lady, to make her like a
raging lion ?"

"I cannot tell ; but oh, Dorothy ! I feel we
are in a sad plight," exclaimed Maud.　And
wearied and worn out, exhausted by her own
fruitless, endless conjectures, and debilitated by

her imprisonment and want of fresh air, the poor girl sank on her knees by Dorothy's side, and hiding her face in her humble friend's lap, burst into an unusual fit of crying.

"Husht! husht, me honeybird!" said the good woman, fairly at her wits' end to soothe her beloved mistress, and to conceal her own increasing fears. "If I could but get word of that illegant gentleman, Master Monteiro. See now, my darling! if I can get out any way to-morrow, may I go and speak to him?"

"Yes, yes, Dorothy! Anything rather than this terrible uncertainty."

"I wonder if that little black creature is sent to the right about like poor Chifferil? I think he must be! As sure as he was roaming the house, he would have been thrusting in his little black head under the tea-tray or Cicely's arm!"

"Surely Lady Helmsford would never send him away?"

In somewhat disjointed and aimless talk, with frequent long pauses, the evening wore away, Dorothy's evident depression weighing heavily on her mistress. Just before they retired for the night, Mistress Beville herself brought a short note, written in evident haste and uneasiness, and signed E. Helmsford. "I, too, am anxious to see you. To-morrow, between twelve and one, I shall visit you. We can then arrange our future plans."

"Pray thank Lady Helmsford for me," cried Maud. "Say I await her with impatience."

"And an illegant story it will be for my lady, the Baroness Langdale, to tell at Court, how she was locked up by her own aunt, and Mistress Beville the jailer!" said Dorothy, with a curtsy.

"We have good reasons for what we do," quoth Beville, with an imperturbable air. "And mayhap your lady will thank us yet. I wish you good-evening, madam."

"Well, dear Dorothy," exclaimed Maud, as Beville closed and locked the door, "this looks well. At last I shall see my aunt!

Perhaps she has some better reason than we wot of for mewing me up thus."

"There's neither better nor best in it at all," said Dorothy sententiously; "only bad and worse."

CHAPTER VI.

T cock-crow next morning, Maud and
her faithful nurse were awoke by
the sounds of movement in the
house—the hauling to and fro as of
boxes and packages, the tramp of feet. Their
breakfast was brought by a young woman
Maud had never seen before, and who replied
to Dorothy's eager queries by saying shortly,
that the noise and disturbance was caused by
preparations for the departure of Mistress
Sparrow with Mab and Tab, and the greater
portion of my lady's luggage, as she was to
precede my lady by a day or two on their
journey to the coast.

Although disturbed by this intelligence, Maud still believed that all would be satisfactorily explained by Lady Helmsford in their fast approaching interview; yet her heart sank as the hour appointed drew near.

"You must stay in the room unless my aunt desires you to leave it," said Maud to her ally.

"To be sure I will; and if I go, I'll not go far," with a knowing look at the door leading to their bed-chamber.

Almost before the appointed hour the key turned in the lock, and Lady Helmsford entered, with a quick, firm step. She was in full morning dress—a sacque of crimson and black brocade, a dark green lutestring petticoat, a Mechlin lace cap and lappets; her cheeks brilliant with rouge; her eyes sparkling with almost metallic brightness.

"I suppose I am in deepest disgrace for thus incarcerating you, Maud! However, you will understand my motives better by-and-by." She smiled a curious hard, sneering smile—a smile that completed the uneasiness with which her look, and voice, and manner inspired her niece.

"Madam, I am deeply indignant at being thus arbitrarily imprisoned for no fault that I am aware of. I have also suffered great anxiety as to what is to become of me. Speak, I pray you! Are you going to start for France, and leave me — to my fate?"

"I give you your choice, Maud. Come with me, and you shall have much pleasure; or stay to know the upshot of your suit to the King."

"But, madam, with whom am I to remain? I know no protector save yourself, who seem to renounce me. I am, of course, desirous to know when Don Juan di Monteiro is to see His Majesty, and to learn the result of the interview."

"And I leave for France to-morrow morning. I have urgent reasons for not delaying my journey. Pooh, child! come with me! ten to one if your suit prospers."

"How?" cried Maud, stepping back with much surprise; "'tis scarce a week since you spoke of my claims as certain to be acknowledged."

" Much has happened to change my views," returned Lady Helmsford moodily. " However, if you are resolved to stay, there is this empty house at your service ; or you can seek sanctuary with your excellent guardian."

" You mock me !" said Maud, the tears springing to her eyes at these words, and the tone in which they were spoken. " One would be as bad as the other. You gone, I should not be left a free agent for twenty-four hours."

" Nay ! scarce for twenty-four hours," remarked the Countess dryly.

" Ah, madam !" cried Maud, clasping her hands, and drawing nearer, " I am very friendless ; do not desert me ! If I have offended, 'twas in ignorance ; surely I have not erred past forgiveness ?"

" Sure, mee lady, you'd never go for to forsake your sister's only child !" exclaimed Dorothy, in a voice that trembled with rage and fear.

" Silence, woman !" said Lady Helmsford,

turning on her a lightning gleam of fury
shining out from behind the mask into which
she had composed her face.

"There remains yet an alternative," she
went on, resuming the carefully-modulated
tone in which she had before spoken;
"one which you will perhaps prefer. Don
Juan di Monteiro visited me yesterday,
and, on hearing my plans, informed me
he had provided a safe and honourable
asylum with some friends of his own."

While she spoke, a deep blush spread over
Maud's cheek.

"Indeed, madam, he is most considerate!
But—but would you not postpone your
journey a day or two rather than throw me
on the protection of a gentleman who has
already shown me so much generosity? Situated as I am, I would fain avoid further
obligations to him."

Maud spoke imploringly.

"I doubt not he will induce you to repay
him amply," said Lady Helmsford, with a
harsh laugh. "No, Mistress Langley, circumstances, compared to which your delicate

scruples are of small account, oblige me to leave London to-morrow."

Maud's countenance fell, the colour faded from her face.

"Well! I'm sure my young lady would be safe and well enough with any friend Mr. Monteiro recommends," quoth Dorothy, who, by some not very clear line of reasoning, or more probably some instinctive impulse, had energetically adopted Monteiro's side.

The Countess did not heed her.

"And where does Don Monteiro design to place me?" asked Maud, with quivering lips, and by a strong effort holding back the tears which pride would not allow her to shed.

"That I cannot tell," returned Lady Helmsford. "In short, Don Juan spoke rudely and unadvisedly, seeming sure of seeing the King to-morrow or next day; certain of success, and therefore insolent. We parted angrily. But I will send and ask him where he means to bestow. you, and say you had better be removed to-day."

"To-day, madam!" said Maud faintly, clasping her hands.

The Countess looked at her scornfully.

"So you are reluctant to meet your husband," she said; "the husband you will neither accept nor renounce. Once more I offer the choice : accompany me, or stay with him !"

Something she could not define of hatred and scorn in Lady Helmsford's voice and manner chilled and revolted Maud.

"I have decided, madam," she exclaimed quickly. "Heaven forbid I trespassed for an unnecessary hour on protection reluctantly extended. Ascertain where Don Juan di Monteiro means to bestow me, and I will relieve you of my presence."

The Countess kept silence for a moment, gazing fixedly at her niece.

"It is well," she said at last slowly; "write to your obliging bridegroom, and I will send your billet. I am somewhat surprised he has not already been here. Has your woman packed your boxes ?"

"Partly, my lady," answered Dorothy, who felt unspeakably anxious to see her mistress safe out of Lady Helmsford's hands, for that lady's altered manner impressed her painfully. "Half an hour will finish them, and, my lady, if you like I can take my lady's—my young lady's message to the gentleman."

A curious sardonic smile curled Lady Helmsford's lip. "You are a prudent woman, and a faithful follower, Mistress Dorothy," she said ; "it shall be as you propose."

"Barring I don't know the way," returned Dorothy, ruefully rubbing her nose.

"Oh, we can supply a guide. Well, then, *dear* niece, write your billet ; in half an hour I shall desire one of the men to be ready to lead your woman to the Don's lodgings."

"Ah ! my aunt," cried Maud, stung by the tone in which the Countess had said "dear niece," and seeing that she turned as if to leave the room—"do not go thus ; although you are cruel now, you *have* been good and generous ! I have never knowingly done aught to merit your anger. Why—why are you so bitter ?"

"Bitter—I am tenderness itself compared to the bitter cup of duplicity and ingratitude *you* have held to my lips !" What glamour have you thrown over Juan di Monteiro to make him false as yourself?"

"Nay, you are indeed unjust," cried Maud, "I cannot prevent Monsieur di Monteiro's fancy or prepossession—or what you will. I have done my best to repress it, believe me; and perhaps, after he has accomplished his friendly mission, we may never meet again."

"How dare you mock me with so monstrous a falsehood! you value Juan's love so lightly, that you care only to repress it? Girl! the very way in which you hesitate to throw yourself on your lover's protection, proves you fear your own heart! Before a week is over you will be his, and then you will learn how much of truth or tenderness a man like Monteiro has for a woman he can legally claim!"

The suppressed fury of Lady Helmsford's tones made her hearers shiver; as she ceased speaking she turned away, and left the room rapidly—not forgetting, however, to turn the key, after closing the door with some violence behind her.

"Don't you shake and tremble so, mavourneen," cried Dorothy, clasping her young mistress in her arms. " Keep up your heart ; if you lose courage now, you may lose everything !"

" But, Dorothy," clinging to her and scarce able to subdue the shivering that shook her frame, " what has turned Lady Helmsford so cruelly against me ? what *have* I done ?"

" Faith, the worst thing one woman could do to another ? You have taken the man she doted on from her."

" I cannot bear to think it !"

" Ah ! never you mind ! my lady is one of those that don't stick at a trifle, and have their little fancies. The Spanish gentleman has just shown her he cares more for the tie of your slipper than the best kiss *she* could give him ! I'll thank God and the blessed saints when you are safe out of the house, mee jewil ! Let me go pack the mails, while you write. Ah ! I wish that civil-spoken gentleman was English, and—"

" He is, Dorothy," interrupted . Maud, still clasping her good friend, and impelled by a true instinct to trust her with Monteiro's secret. " Never breathe what I am about to

say. But he is English, and of my own
blood; he is Rupert Langley, my father's
first cousin, and his errand in London is to
save me from my uncle."

" Oh! blessed hour! You don't mean it!
Are ye sure, mee darling?"

" I am, dear nurse! he holds letters from
my father. He knows the family history! I
I am *quite* sure!"

" Then I will go seek him with a heart and
a half—does my lady know this?"

" No, Dorothy! and you must guard the
secret!"

" I will so! Faith, all will go right now!
Here's the pen and paper, mavourneen!"

" No, Dorothy! I cannot write to my
kinsman. He knows you; a message will do
as well. Tell him all my aunt says (I mean
of her departure), and the necessity of my
seeking shelter elsewhere; beg him to believe
it is my only chance of escaping John Langley."

" Lave it all to me," returned Dorothy,
with her head in a box. "*I'll* speak to him,
never fear!"

Within the specified half-hour Mistress Beville made her appearance. " Mistress Dorothy," she said, " if you are ready, my lady says there is a coach at the door to take you on your errand."

" I'll come in ten minutes," replied Dorothy, rising from her knees.

" Are Mistress Langley's packages ready ?"

" All but turning the keys, which I'm sure, if there is any good in practice, you're equal to do !" returned Dorothy with a sneer.

" You will come down, then, when you are ready," said Beville, unmoved, and left the room, wonderful to relate, without locking the door after her.

" Well, well," exclaimed Dorothy, who was tying on her hood, and otherwise preparing to go out; " our troubles are nearly over ; won't I get a hearty welcome where I am going ? No matter."

" And you will come back as soon as ever you can ! Dear kind Dorothy," cried Maud, kissing and clinging to her, " I cannot tell you the sort of despair I feel at letting you go even for an hour ! Come back quickly ! and no matter how humble the shelter my—my— cousin has found for me, I will gladly abide there."

" Just lave it all to me, and keep up your heart.   I'll come back as quick as ever I can ! and I'll go bail mee gentleman will come fetch you himself," added Dorothy, with a knowing nod.

" No, no ! I would much rather not.   I would, indeed," repeated Maud, following her to the door.

The time that ensued wore on heavily and nervously for Maud, who strove to employ herself by looking into the various drawers and wardrobes, and adding any stray for- gotten articles she found therein to the mails already filled by Dorothy's dexterous hands, and then crouching on a footstool over the embers of the decaying fire, she waited, in an anxious, yet dreamy state of mind, for her nurse's return.

Meantime, when Dorothy descended, she met Mistress Letitia Sparrow in the hall, who expressed much pleasure at having an oppor- tunity of bidding her adieu.

"Ah! will you try to go up and stay a while with mee poor darlin' young lady? I know she'll be fretting all alone by herself there; and I'll be. back soon."

"I will try, good Mistress Dorothy, but indeed I dare not promise. I am sure I know not what is come to the house, everything seems topsy-turvy! My lady is that strange—so hurried with her preparations one minute, and ready to put them aside the next. Is Mistress Langley coming with us to Paris?"

"How can I—" began Dorothy, when she was cut short by the sharp accents of Beville.

"Mistress Sparrow," they called out, "my lady asks for you, you had better come at once."

Mistress Sparrow hurried away. The porter threw wide the door, a hackney coach stood at the entrance, a respectable-looking serving-man in plain livery (but not my lady's colours) held the coach door open.

"You are to take me to Don Monteiro's lodgings," said Dorothy, with what she considered an imposing air. "Do you know where he lives?"

"Yes, madam," he replied respectfully.

"Well, go the shortest way," remarked Dorothy, stepping into the vehicle. The man mounted beside the coachman, who drove off directly at a pretty good pace. As the coach turned into Charles Street, D'Arcy entered the square from Pall Mall.

Monteiro, although fully believing the Countess's professions of partial reconciliation and good faith, and determined to keep his promise not to interfere with her, even by a visit of inquiry during the day that intervened between their last interview and his anticipated presentation to the King, could not subdue an uneasy feeling which induced him to send D'Arcy with polite inquiries as to Lady Helmsford's health, and directions to pick up any stray information he could without point-blank interrogations. Above all, he was not to ask for Gomez, though he might speak to him if he happened to be in the hall. Thus warned, D'Arcy approached the enemy.

"Her ladyship is better this morning," was the porter's reply to D'Arcy's queries; "but too unwell and too much occupied to see any one."

"Ay! just so," said D'Arcy. "And Mistress Langley and the rest?"

"Mistress Langley has not been downstairs or out for a long time; but her woman has just now gone forth to shop or some such thing. I heard her tell Mistress Sparrow as she went by, that her mistress would be lonesome while she was out, but that she would be back soon."

"Oh! what a grand place you have here! No end of company too, I suppose."

"Not for the last few days; it has been like a city of the dead! Don Juan di Monteiro was here about this time yesterday, and by my troth! not a soul, gentle or simple, has crossed the threshold since! I don't know when such a thing happened before; and my lady never left her own apartments since the day before yesterday."

"Faith, she must be mighty ill," observed D'Arcy; "and when does she start for Paris?"

"I do not know—I don't think the day is fixed yet."

"Well, I will not trouble you any more. Good-day to you," and D'Arcy stalked back to give a faithful report of this conversation, from which Monteiro derived great satisfaction.

If Dorothy, the devoted Dorothy, was going out freely and contentedly on some small mission, all was well. She would not quit her beloved mistress even for an hour, were she not convinced of her safety. Her speech with Mistress Sparrow also showed a relaxation of the Lady Helmsford's wrath and severity. So with his apprehensions set at rest, Monteiro prepared for the event of to-morrow.

While Monteiro thus consoled himself, time went on slowly for poor Maud. About an hour and a half after Dorothy had left dinner was brought in, and Maud had hardly finished the pretence of eating it when Mistress Sparrow made her appearance.

It seemed so long since the poor little *dame*

de compagnie had paid her a visit, and the sight of a friendly face was so welcome in her solitude, that Maud, yielding to her kindly impulse, kissed the well-rouged cheek with due caution.

" I am so glad to see you, Mistress Sparrow ; my good Dorothy has left me for a while, but I marvel she is not back again."

"Indeed, my dear young lady, I should have come to visit you before had I not been strictly forbidden. I grieve to see you so pallid ; but the charming air of *la belle France* will soon bring back your roses. You accompany us, do you not ?"

" No, good Mistress Sparrow, I think not !"

" Dear, dear ! then I must say adieu now, for I leave immediately. Ah me ! but I am sorry to bid you good-bye ! you have ever been so kind and gentle." The tears stood in poor Letitia's eyes as she spoke.

"I trust we shall meet again," said Maud, tenderly taking her hand.

" But I am forgetting myself," cried Mistress Sparrow, with a sudden start. " My

lady has sent me to fetch you ; she has a message, I think, from Mistress Dorothy."

"Indeed ! Oh, let us go to her at once ;
'tis strange though that Dorothy has not returned."

So saying, Maud followed Mistress Sparrow,
and soon outstripped her in her half-fearful
curiosity and eagerness.

"My lady is in her study," cried Letitia.

Maud tapped at the door.

"Come in," said the Countess. She was
sitting at her writing-table looking at a piece
of rather crumpled paper, on which several
lines were traced. "This is from your
woman," she said, as Maud entered and stood
before her. "She writes—'I have seen
Master di Monteiro, he is much engaged or
would bear this himself. This is a proper
place, the house of a respectable Spaniard,
whose wife is English. I stay to make all
ready and to receive my young mistress when
it pleases her to come.—I am your ladyship's
obedient servant, Dorothy.' There," concluded Lady Helmsford, handing her the paper,
"I suppose you know your woman's writing ?"

" I can scarce say I do ; but she *can* write.
I think she has found some one to write for
her—see what a scrawl her name is compared
to the rest. But I am right glad she has
found a refuge for me. I would fain go there
as soon as possible, and so relieve your ladyship of a troublesome charge."

" 'Tis best so," returned Lady Helmsford,
who spoke more gently than when Maud saw
her a couple of hours before, and looked down
upon her blotting-book while she spoke.
" See, the letter is dated from ' Bow Street,'
a respectable place enough, though scarce in
the repute it once had. Still——" she hesitated ; Maud preserved a respectful silence.
" I know what will be the best plan," resumed the Countess, with a sort of effort, and
slowly raising her eyes till they met those of
her niece. " Sparrow will start with some of
the baggage almost directly. She can take
you *en route*, and see you safely to your destination."

" 'Tis well thought of, madam," said Maud
gladly.

"Go, then, and make your preparations,"

returned the Countess, again averting her eyes. "I will give directions to my people —and—and—I will see you ere you start."

Mistress Sparrow, who had entered with Maud but stood respectfully in the background, made a little step forward with a pleased expression on her countenance: "Yes, Sparrow, go with Mistress Langley; assist her to dress. Go!"

Lady Helmsford waved them away somewhat impatiently.

"Nay! I am indeed fortunate to have a little more of your company," quoth Letitia, as they re-entered Maud's sitting-room, where they found one of the footmen already removing the boxes which Dorothy had packed.

"I wish you were to be with us, my dear young lady; and methinks, from her looks and tones, my lady the Countess is grieved to part with you!"

"And perhaps, also, for treating me so ill," replied Maud. "Ah, Mistress Sparrow! how near I have been to loving my aunt; she is so grand and beautiful! Why has she been so cruel and unjust, and thrust me from her?"

"She is hard to deal with at times! Still a grand lady to serve. I could scarce find such a home elsewhere. The world is a cold place, dear Mistress Langley, to an unprovided gentlewoman like myself; therefore, if I seem somewhat subservient to my lady at times, you must not despise me!"

"God forbid!" said Maud gently. "Why should I wish you to contradict my aunt? but I must find my hat and cloak."

Mistress Sparrow gladly assisted in the operation of attiring the young lady, who soon donned her black silk furbelowed scarf, and small hat, tied with violet ribbon and decorated with velvet pansies; drawing on her well-fitting many-buttoned grey gloves, and laying her cardinal cloak ready to wrap round her, for the days were yet chill, she declared herself ready. Mistress Sparrow went to seek her outdoor garments, and Maud stood by the fireplace gazing at the room which had been her home for nearly three months, and from which she was going forth into an unknown world.

What alternations of hope and fear she had

experienced there! what sharp pain and disappointment, with faint trembling gleams of half-dreaded sweetness, when she thought of Rupert her cousin—her avowed lover, whom she at once feared yet trusted! Young and unlearned in life's bitter lore as she was, she felt that his love for her was the cause of her aunt's harshness; but if Rupert had been false to Lady Helmsford, how could she trust him? Might not the Countess have been misled by her own fancy, her own imperious will? Monteiro or Rupert could not be false! —impetuous, hasty, over-bold, perhaps, but not false; his frank clear eyes seemed to smile upon her as she thought. Moreover, her sound natural sense suggested that had there been any baseness, of which Lady Helmsford could with a shadow of truth accuse him, she would have done so. What she had said was formless and vague. But Maud scarce acknowledged to her heart how disappointed she felt that Monteiro had not come himself to escort her to the asylum he had provided. She had at first shrunk from the embarrassment of leaving her aunt's house under his protection; but now it seemed unkind of him not to come. On the whole, however, she felt more hopeful and at rest than she had done for many days, and was quite satisfied when Mistress Sparrow again summoned her to bid farewell to her prison.

" The coach waits," said the *dame de compagnie;* " it is full time I were on my road."

Maud therefore, mindful of Lady Helmsford's wish to see her once more, descended to the dressing-room, where she found her aunt standing near the windows, as if arrested in pacing to and fro.

" I come to bid you adieu, madam," said Maud, in unsteady accents, seeing her aunt kept silence. The idea of parting in this cold unfriendly manner affected her keenly; still the Countess does not speak. " You have been most generous to me, you afforded me help in time of sore need; and if you now show me a harsher mood, believe me when I am away I will only remember your happier aspect with gratitude. Give me your hand before I go."

" Do not ask me, Maud !" exclaimed Lady Helmsford in a curious smothered voice. " I cannot now—but—but, child, hereafter—if you are in difficulties, if he who will be your husband ill-treats you, come to me, and I will aid you to the utmost of my power. Remember this, Maud !"

"Indeed, madam ; I hope I may never be driven to so sad a strait."

"Nevertheless, *remember*," repeated Lady Helmsford. " Now, go ; Sparrow should have been on the road more than an hour ago ; go !"

Thus repulsed, Maud curtsied obediently, though much struck by her aunt's tone, and withdrew.

In the hall was some disorder and litter of straw, as if packages had been carried through ; and at the door stood a large carriage, laden with luggage, to which were attached four post-horses. Everything being ready, directly Maud and Mistress Sparrow took their places therein, and a sober elderly man—the "*locum tenens*," Letitia whispered, for Chifferil—with bows and apologies, followed them, the lumbering vehicle was put in motion, and started at a tolerable pace, making for the direction of Long Acre, whereat Mistress Sparrow expressed her gratification, as the condition of the Strand was such that she declared it inevitably entailed sore bones to travel along it. " 'Tis also the best way to Bow Street," she added, and then proceeded to chatter volubly about her regret to part with Mistress Langley; of the princely grandeur in which my lady the Countess travelled, always with three carriages, which necessitated the despatch of a part of the retinue a day in advance, by reason of difficulties connected with a supply of post-horses, etc., etc. Maud was thankful to be spared the trouble of answering ; lost in her own thoughts, which her parting with her aunt rendered both sad and troubled, she did not give much heed to the streets they passed, and in her ignorance of the great capital could form no idea of the distance or position of the place to which they were journeying

At length the motion of the carriage and the clatter of Letitia's tongue ceased together. Maud looked up. The coach had stopped in a grave-looking street, opposite a solemn mansion of red brick, with stone copings—a house that seemed in some odd way known to her.

"Why! what are they stopping for?" cried Letitia; "this is Great Queen Street."

"By her ladyship's commands," said the new secretary, who had not hitherto spoken.

A sudden terror fell on Maud; the next instant the house-door flew open, and she beheld a respectable solid-looking serving-man, and beyond him, standing bareheaded in the entrance, as though at home, her uncle, John Langley, with a grim smile on his countenance. Maud's heart seemed to die within her.

"There must be some mistake," she said with white trembling lips. "Lady Helmsford desired that I should be conveyed to Bow Street where my woman Dorothy awaits me."

"Pardon me, madam," replied the secretary, who had already alighted, "the last order from the Countess was to place you under the care of your good guardian there."

Mistress Sparrow burst into violent weeping. " I knew naught of it, believe me! I knew naught," she repeated.

" 'Tis indeed the cruellest treachery," cried Maud, indignation mastering fear for the moment. " I will not leave the coach! Surely I am a free agent. I demand to be taken——"

The words died on her lips. To whom could she go? She feared to name Monteiro lest she might bring him into danger, and even if she had, would it avail? Ah, why, why was he not there to shield her? Had *he*, too, forsaken her?

" Scarcely a free agent while under age, fair niece," said Langley, stepping forward and holding out his hand with ceremonious polite- ness to assist her in alighting. " Be advised ; your noble aunt restores you to my custody, and I am determined you shall return to my house. Make no unseemly resistance, 'twill but make matters worse. What is the will of one feeble, peevish girl against mine ?"

Maud's pride enabled her to suppress an impulse to scream aloud in her hopeless anguish. She had a dim feeling that her guardian might gloat over an impotent resistance, her sensitive delicacy shrank from the possibility that rude hands might touch her—all this, and much more, flashed along the electric lines of thought even while her uncle spoke. Yes! the only course left to her weakness was submission, and then she would see Dorothy, who was no doubt entrapped like herself.

When Langley ceased speaking, a moment's dead silence fell upon them all, broken only by poor Letitia's sobs.

"You are within your rights," said Maud at length, very distinctly and calmly, calm with the stillness of despair, while she turned deadly white. "I will descend." Then turning to Mistress Sparrow she pressed her hand. "I in nowise blame you," she said aloud; then, stooping as though to kiss her cheek, whispered, "For God's sake contrive to let Don Monteiro know—he lodges in Salisbury Street, Strand—for God's sake!"

"I will, I will!" muttered the terrified afflicted *dame de compagnie.*

Maud, again pressing her hand, stepped lightly from the carriage without touching her uncle's outstretched arm.

The servant threw open the dining-room door, and Maud walked mechanically into that dreary apartment.

In a minute or two she heard the rumble of the coach as it drove away, and felt herself doomed and powerless; the next, John Langley entered and stood face to face with his niece.

Maud Langley was a woman of no common character, and it was rapidly developing. Under a soft, tender, beauty-loving, restful surface, lay a store of courage, of common sense, of readiness to make the best of things, of purest loyalty ; and with these the blessed gift of self-control, the power to mask her feelings, with which merciful nature, by her admirable system of compensations, arms the weaker sex. And now, though dizzy with this sudden revelation of her aunt's black treachery, she strove, with all the mental force she could rally, to understand and grapple with her position. She looked fully, but not de-

fiantly into her guardian's eyes till, with a
curious sense of humiliation, he averted his;
and forced by her silence into speech, he
said:

"'Tis to be regretted, young mistress, that
your reluctance to return to the shelter of
your guardian's roof necessitated something
of stratagem."

" Now I *am* here, sir, what is your will respecting me ?"

" Listen, Maud," he returned, trying with
small success to speak pleasantly ; " I wish to
deal kindly and fairly by you ! I am vexed
and wounded by your determined rejection of
my son ; but I am resolved not to force you
into a marriage which might embitter his life.
He does not share my views—the foolish
boy is infatuated by you ! He has been
sick to death from this silly passion. I
have therefore removed him, lest he might
annoy you. He is now far away ; to-morrow
I intend to send you under safe escort to
Langdale. I cannot myself accompany you,
as I have business in another direction ; but
so far as in me lies I shall prevent Harold

having access to, or in any way molesting you.
I wonder he hath not more pride than to
persevere in spite of so many rebuffs."

" If such are your intentions, sir," said
Maud, still looking very keenly at him,
" you leave me no cause for wishing to quit
your care—at any rate for the present! I
regret to hear my cousin is still indisposed,
although I do not for a moment believe that
I have any share in causing his suffering—on
this point either you deceive yourself, or *he*
deceives you."

" Had my Lady Helmsford been faithful to
her engagement, and truly favoured Harold's
suit, instead of permitting every honey-
tongued, empty-headed fine gentleman of her
following access to you, you would have
thought more favourably of Harold's suit; but
it is useless and unworthy of repine, though
I marvel that a young woman, in some ways
sufficiently sensible, cannot see the advan-
tages of such a union !"

In fact Langley was much relieved by his
niece's acquiescence. Outcries and a scene,
such as he had anticipated, would have

created an enormous scandal, and thus tempo-
rarily gratified, he told himself that his feelings
towards his niece would have been friendly
—nay, fatherly—had she not been contu-
macious, contemptuous, and irreligiously re-
bellious, in that she dared to cross his will
and upset the plan he had so admirably
arranged for his own and his son's benefit.

"Let us say no more on the subject," returned Maud. "Permit me to go to my own
room, where I suppose I shall find my good
Dorothy."

She longed to be free from the presence of
one she at once feared and despised.

"Your former apartment is prepared for
you; but Mistress Dorothy is not here—she
did not accompany you?"

At this further evidence of a deep-laid
plot Maud's courage and composure almost
failed.

"Where—where can poor Dorothy be?"
she exclaimed. "What terror she must be
in, separated from me in this great, awful
city! Ah! my uncle! do send for her—do
find her!"

"Well, niece!" replied Langley with a grim smile, "how came you to part with this valued attendant?"

Maud paused for a moment of rapid thought. How much did her uncle know of Monteiro's scheme? at any rate she must not admit too much.

"Lady Helmsford sent her on an errand," she said faintly. Again the grim smile passed over Langley's face, this time tinged with triumph.

"I know the errand, mistress," he said dryly; "my Lady Helmsford was good enough to confide to me some of the difficulties she has had to contend with concerning you— and the bold pretension of this Spanish adventurer was no trifling matter! She should never have exposed you to his advances! However, you will see *him* no more, *that* I am resolved. Strange, that you should be more inclined to favour one so utterly unknown than a kinsman!"

These last words showed Maud that, at least, the truth of Monteiro's lineage was unknown; she felt that her own danger and

49

difficulty would be increased were she to reveal it, apart from the deadly hatred to which she would expose him.

"Then what has become of Dorothy? I am sure, sir, you know! do, I beseech you, restore her to me!"

"I will," replied Langley, with a slight bow or bend of the head, intended to show extreme graciousness. "I have arranged that she shall join you to-morrow evening at the first stage of your journey to Langdale; does that content you, fair mistress?"

"It must," replied Maud coldly. "Now may I seek my own room?"

"Certainly! You will there find the attendant I have provided. I hope for the pleasure of your company at dinner?"

"I have dined," said Maud; "and my company would give you but scant pleasure; suffer me to remain in my chamber?"

To this Langley thought it best to agree, and Maud, at last, escaped. A staid but stern-looking female received her with a respectful curtsy, but met the anxious, entreating glance which the young lady cast upon her with a fixed and threatening eye, expressive of the unfriendly watchfulness wherewith the keepers of the insane cow their charges ; there was nothing to be hoped from her—she was an enemy to be guarded against.

Maud mechanically laid aside her outdoor wraps, accepting the help of her uncongenial attendant; then, with another look at her face, she tried what speech would do to break the spell the woman's presence seemed to work upon her.

" Are you to accompany me on my journey to-morrow ?"

" I believe so, madam."

" At what hour are we to set out ?"

" I know not, madam," very stiffly conveying " I will not tell."

Maud felt there was nothing to be won from her.

" I am somewhat weary and indisposed," she said ; " I want nothing more—you may leave me."

" That I must not, madam. I have Mr. Langley's commands not to lose sight of you, till you are safe in the hands of your own woman."

"It is useless to dispute his will now," returned Maud quietly, though her heart beat fast with increasing fear and anger at this indication of the tenacious grasp he had laid upon her. "May I have a book to pass the weary hours till 'tis time to sleep?"

The woman rang, and another younger person, whom Maud remembered when she had before been imprisoned in the same sombre apartments, came at the summons.

"Good-day to you, Susan," said Maud, with her usual kindly courtesy.

"I am main glad to see your ladyship," replied the woman cordially, and dropping a curtsy.

"You must speak to me, not to Mistress Langley," said Maud's keeper. "The young lady asks for a book. Do you wish any particular book, madam?"

"No—anything Mr. Langley chooses."

Susan disappeared, and soon returned with a volume of "Waller's Poems." With this in her hand to serve as a shelter to her face,

Maud settled herself in an un-easy chair, and gave herself up to intense, though un-connected thought.

She was indeed entrapped. Her one chance of deliverance lay in poor Mistress Sparrow ! of her good-will Maud never doubted; but she was timid, and not very clear-headed; was she capable of conveying a warning to Monteiro ? and, even if she did, how would he contrive to liberate her ? This last question, however, did not trouble her much; she felt sure he would manage to set her free. How could Lady Helmsford have been so cruelly treacherous—so regardless of all womanly sympathy ! The tears coursed plentifully down Maud's cheeks and fell on her book, as she thought of her kinswoman's baseness— of her own isolated, forlorn condition ! Her only friend on earth, beside her poor, helpless, lost Dorothy, was Monteiro; and towards him she felt, at any rate, complete trust, she would have gone anywhere with him; done anything he told her, confident that he was incapable of using any opportunity save for her own advantage. But young as she was,

Maud knew that if she accepted his assistance, and the necessities of her flight obliged
her to remain with him alone, she would be
in the eyes of the world his wife *de facto*,
however chivalrous his generosity might be;
and from this tremendous decision for her
whole life she still shrank, even while she
thought of Monteiro with grateful tenderness,
and longed with unspeakable longing to see
his frank, kind face, and to feel that he stood
between her and her foes.   His possible
entanglement with the Countess, too, seemed
of less formidable proportions as Maud re-
flected that it was Monteiro's fidelity to herself that had no doubt drawn upon her the
bitterness which prompted her aunt's cruelty.
But how fatal it all was!   How much of
John Langley's protestations dare she believe? and poor, dear Dorothy! what misery
and agony was she not now enduring! and
would she indeed find her on her way to
Langdale?

It was hard, with all these thoughts
crowding and jostling each other in her
strained heart and busy brain, to keep up the

semblance of reading, and suppress the uneasiness that urged her to rise and pace the room, to look from the window, and see, like Sister Ann, if there was any one coming.

But she strove to control herself, she formed earnest inarticulate prayers in her heart, as she counted the hours and half-hours that chimed from some neighbouring church, and waited and waited, in sickening suspense, for the rescue she dared not despair of. Surely Rupert—her husband—would come before night!

Meantime, Mistress Mathews—the sentinel placed over Maud—sat at a respectful distance and knitted.

At seven, Susan brought supper, and, having assisted Mathews to lay it, stayed to wait upon Maud, as Mistress Mathews had her portion served upon a distant table.

Maud, hoping to keep up her own strength, and by it her courage, attempted to eat ; but revolted from food.

" Lawk, mistress !" cried Susan to Maud's jailer ; " how deadly my young lady looks ! she cannot eat a bit !"

"Fetch some wine," said Mathews, rising quickly from her supper. "Do you feel faint, madam ?"

"By no means," replied Maud, struggling gallantly with the horrible sinking of the heart which oppressed her; "but I will gladly take some wine."

A glass of John Langley's famous Burgundy greatly revived her; she was even able to eat a little afterwards.

Then she resumed her watch by the fire, while Mathews nodded over her knitting, and gave frequent hints that Mistress Langley would be better abed. But they were thrown away.

Affecting deep interest in her book, Maud contrived to prolong the sitting till nearly eleven o'clock—hoping, listening, for some signs of rescue; but in vain. So at last she consented to go to bed, and, utterly exhausted, fell asleep sooner than she expected.

It was, however, but a dream-haunted slumber that fell upon her. All the terror, and pain, and indignation of the past day came back to her in the strange, distorted forms which present themselves to semi-consciousness ; and then her waking was terrible.

While Maud watched, Langley was busy with his papers and calculations.

A man on horseback came to the door, and sent in word that he bore a message from Lord Berkeley. He was admitted, and stayed more than half an hour. When he departed, Mr. Langley too called for wine—a most unusual demand from him.

" I am obliged to meet my lord at a place nigh Roehampton," said Langley to his servant, as he filled his glass, " to meet him to-morrow afternoon ; so I cannot accompany my niece the first stage of her journey, as I intended."

The servant merely said, " Indeed, sir !" but he thought it passing strange that an Admiralty messenger should be masked.

Soon after Langley himself retired, and silence settled down upon the house.

Next morning Maud's breakfast was served in her room, and she was informed that some time about noon they were to start on their long, toilsome journey to the South Coast. Maud thought it somewhat late ; but said nothing, as every moment's delay seemed to give her a little further chance of deliverance.

But time wore on, and it was two o'clock before word was brought to Mistress Langley that all was prepared, and the carriage awaited her.

Closely followed by her duenna, she descended and found John Langley in the hall. He wore a riding-dress and boots.

" I am obliged to bid you adieu here, fair niece," he said. " Business takes me elsewhere, but I have provided for your safety."

Indeed there were two stout men well armed on horseback, and a servant in the Langley livery on the box, besides the postillions. " You will follow the road through Chelsea to the ferry at Battersea, another coach awaits you at the farther side of the river, and there you will find your favourite, Mistress Dorothy. I am going by the Horse Ferry ; ere long I hope to visit you at Langdale. Adieu then, young mistress ; you

may yet regret your wilfulness and contra--
diction."

There was something painful and deadly in
the sort of forced smile with which Langley
spoke these words. And Maud, now plunged
into the apathy of despair, not even reassured
by the promise of meeting Dorothy, answered
him never a word ; she bent her head and let
him take her cold limp hand to lead her to
the carriage.

As soon as the woman called Mathews
took her place beside her, the vehicle was put
in motion, the armed men placed themselves
on either side, and they drove slowly away into
Lincoln Fields and Holborn, directing their
way to Uxbridge Road.

But Maud looked from the window in vain ;
the road they travelled and the faces they
passed were alike unknown. Overpowered
by a sense of her own impotence she leant
back out of sight, and giving herself up sunk
into a sort of stupor.

The houses became fewer and fewer. Long
stretches of market gardens, already beginning
to be a source of wealth, succeeded, a country

place or two, and then wild dreary open
marshy fields and utter loneliness.

"We must be near the river now, I should
think," said Mistress Mathews, who had been
less taciturn than on the previous day. "'Tis
a rare lonesome place. I would we were at
the Ferry. There, madam, I am to give over
my charge of you to an attendant of your own,
a Mistress Dorothy."

"Then it is true," said Maud, reviving a
little. "I scarce believed Master Langley's
assurances."

"True enough," repeated Mathews, looking from the window. "But goodness! heart
alive! who be these men that seem drawn up
to stop our way?"

Roused by this exclamation, Maud looked
forth in her turn, and coming round a bend of
the road on horseback, covered with horsemen's cloaks and wearing slouched hats, came
three men, while a fourth followed a little way
behind. "Good Lord deliver us! 'tis a party
of highwaymen! I can see they are masked,"
continues Mathews, clutching Maud—"or,
madam! is it an attempt at rescue? You know

these people ? You will assure them I have treated you with all kindness and respect ?"

" Indeed, I do not know them—yet, pray God they may be coming to my aid !" cried Maud, her hopes once more alight, her heart beating.

" Stand and deliver !" cried one of the horsemen, dashing forward and holding a pistol to the nearest postillion's head ; he and his comrade instantly drew rein, and the coach came suddenly to a standstill. At the same time the men who formed Maud's escort rode up and a sharp fight appeared to proceed ; the horses wheeling and prancing, created vast clouds of dust, men shouted, pistols were fired and swords clashed, while the servant who had sat on the box descended and disappeared.

Within the carriage the two terrified women clung to each other, both believing the attack to be an attempt at rescue ; and the woman Mathews alternately implored Maud's good offices with the victors, and bewailed her probable fate if Master Langley were to believe she was privy to the plan.

Maud, her eyes hidden on her companion's shoulder, listened with mingled terror and expectation. How earnestly she hoped no one would be hurt! How ardently she thirsted for the first sound of Monteiro's voice, for Monteiro must be at the head of the party which disputed their passage.

At last one of the horsemen who had accompanied them was seen riding off at speed; and the man with whom he had been engaged, riding up to the carriage window, took off his hat:

"Be not alarmed, ladies, I beg. This is but an attempt on the-part of true love to deliver captive beauty from the hands of the oppressor. We shall just turn your horses' heads in the direction of a place of safety, where all shall be explained."

He spoke in a fat jovial voice, as through a medium of mashed potatoes.

"Pray, sir," said Maud, looking up now that the fray was over, and "nobody seemed a penny the worse," "who commands this party? I would speak with your leader."

"He will present himself to you, madam,

when we reach the—the abode of bliss—the Karavanserai, whither we are about to proceed."

"And I can tell you the worshipful Mr. Langley will hang you as high as Haman for this day's work," cried the duenna; "you will do well to hide your gallows face! but I will swear to your voice any day, if so be as I can compass your punishment!"

"A thousand thanks, madam, for your friendly intentions. Here! John, Robert, Thomas! by whatever appellation you are known, mount the box once more."

So saying he reined back his horse to admit of the cumbrous vehicle turning, which was accomplished with much difficulty; and as it turned, Maud caught a glimpse of a group of six or seven horsemen clustered together on the sward of a small common or waste, which at that point bordered the road. She scanned them eagerly, though not near enough to see their features; none had the carriage or bearing of Monteiro. Nor would he have permitted a man like the insolent bravo who had just spoken to approach her; but, the cautious

turning having been accomplished, Maud saw
no more.

The man-servant who had accompanied
them from town now approached and en-
treated her not to be alarmed : " All will go
well, madam, believe me !   I soon found
'twere best not to show fight !"

" Ay! so you did, I'il warrant ye for a
pack of cowardly loons ! I will tell Master
Langley how you quitted you of your charge,"
cried Mathews.

" Well, you had best hold your tongue
now," returned the man, with a grin ; and
mounting the coach-box once more, he spoke
to the postillions, who drove on at a quick
pace. Soon they diverged to a side road,
narrow and rutty.

Again Maud's heart sank in despair.   Was
her last state to be worse than the first? What
strange, unknown country was this ? she
thought, as the carriage turned and twined
through rugged lanes and by-roads. Her
companion was voluble in her fear and anger,
but Maud was nearly speechless.

She saw by the keen, sharply bright, level

sunlight, that the day was drawing to a close. She felt she was going farther and farther from human aid.

She noticed that a horseman, of a somewhat superior air, constantly rode at the off-side of the carriage ; and, although masked, there was something familiar to her in his bearing and the turn of his head.

At last the carriage stopped, a gate was opened, and in a few minutes they again drew up at the entrance of a tall, red-brick, melancholy-looking house, surrounded by fir trees and poplars. Some of the windows were stopped up, the shutters of others were closed; altogether it looked the fitting scene for crime.

Here was evidently the end of the journey. The postillion on the leader dismounted, and began to remove his saddle, and the horseman Maud had noticed followed his example, advancing hat in hand ; she observed that one arm was in a sling.

" Let me assist you to descend," he said in a voice she knew too well. " 'Tis a poor place;

but you cannot doubt the heartiness of the welcome, sweet cousin."

"Harold!" she exclaimed, almost fainting; "Harold! why have you brought me here?"

CHAPTER VII.

HILE Maud waited and watched all the long dreary morning with alternations of hope and despair, Monteiro was alert. He rose at an early hour, and despatched his valet with a note to Lady Helmsford—a few lines of polite inquiry—just to keep his mind at rest.

The Countess wrote a gracious reply. All was well, she said. John Langley had made no sign. She was hurrying her preparations, and begged he would call as soon as his interview with the King was over. This was signed his faithful friend, "E. Helmsford," and

50—2

answered its object in keeping Monteiro perfectly quiet and content.

His trust in the Countess was not altogether complete, yet he credited her with too
much judgment, too much regard for her own
character, and too strong a dash of generosity
withal, to permit of his imagining the enormous treachery of which she had been guilty.
Then he had always observed a certain nobility in her pride and wilfulness which blinded
him to the violence of her passion, to the
relentless cruelty which opposition to her
will, or mortification of her vanity, might call
forth.

With a mind at rest then, as regarded
Maud's safety, Monteiro dressed for his presentation to the King, yet not with anticipations of unchequered brightness. A few hours,
and the difficult game he had been playing
would be played out. A few hours, and in
the presence of Sir Stephen Compton, of
Lady Helmsford, perhaps of others, he would
solemnly declare Maud Langley free of any
claim on his part.

Then how would he stand? If the King

were so well disposed as to accept his services, there was still a career before him ; but even so, how long would it be before he should win distinction enough to entitle him—a cadet of the family—to aspire to the hand of the heiress and head of the house ?

Even if Maud was inclined to be gracious, it was his bounden duty not to press his suit. "At least, I suppose so," were his concluding reflections; "though, if she smiles, I am not sure how I shall perform that part of my duty. However, she does not seem very favourably disposed towards me; though 'tis hard to say how much of what that handsome termagant, Lady Helmsford, says is worth belief. After all, love and marriage are not the only objects in life for a man of action. Let me do my devoir this day, confound John Langley, ensure the safety of my sweetest, fairest cousin (I must not think of her as my bride), and then life is surely large enough to afford oblivion and an aftergrowth happiness. At any rate, unless John Langley assassinates me before this afternoon, I shall see Maud, and look into her eyes, and hear her speak, and kiss her hand—perhaps her lips. Faith! she might grant me that much for my services!" On this moment, in truth, all his expectations hinged—beyond it he did not look.

Monteiro, as was natural, was first to arrive at the old gateway, still so familiar to Londoners. He ordered the driver of his coach to draw up and wait. Nor did Sir Stephen keep him long. The handsomely appointed equipage of the accomplished Baronet stopped, and Monteiro received a cordial greeting.

"Step in, my dear sir," cried Sir Stephen. "We are in excellent time; and have you any further tidings of your fair bride? Zounds! my good Monteiro, you must by no means relinquish the vantage-ground your bold stratagem gives you."

"I shall be guided by circumstances, Sir Stephen," replied Monteiro, taking his seat in the carriage, which rolled under the archway and drove in a stately fashion round the carriage sweep, stopping at one of the principal entrances. "I trust it will be convenient for you to accompany me to Lady Helmsford's residence, that I may present you to the young Baroness, after we have seen the King. Lady Helmsford leaves for Paris to-morrow or next day, and would no doubt be pleased to find her niece provided with suitable protection ere she departs."

"Yes, yes ! I will go with you ; but as to protection, take my advice—seek none beyond your own. Who so suitable a protector as her wedded husband ?"

To this Monteiro made no reply, as Sir Stephen was in the act of alighting while he spoke.

A sentinel of the Grenadier Guards was walking up and down, and several servants in the royal livery came to the door to receive the visitors, followed by an usher, who evidently knew Sir Stephen. "My Lord Sunderland and Master Craggs are even now with His Majesty ; but if you and this gentleman will follow me, you can await your turn of audience."

He led them up a wide, short flight of stairs, which Monteiro thought scarcely looked like the principal staircase of a palace. From the landing several doors opened, and, throwing one wide, their conductor led them through a room of moderate size, where a swarthy but good-looking man, in a Turkish dress and large turban, was lounging half asleep on a settee by the fire ; two pages were playing cards in a window-seat, and a couple of German lacqueys were laughing and talking over a letter one seemed reading to the other.

All rose and bowed profoundly as Sir Stephen and his companion passed through to a farther apartment, the door of which was opened by the usher. Here were two or three gentlemen in clerical, civil, and military costumes, the latter garb being worn by a stout portly personage in the uniform of a commanding officer of the Hanoverian Guards.

He hailed the entrance of Sir Stephen by a loud exclamation in German and a slap on the shoulder. The Baronet endured this rough greeting with smiling courtesy; and the others saluted him respectfully.

After a few words, evidently questions respecting Monteiro, towards whom the officer looked with undisguised curiosity.

"Count Bernsdorf desires to be made known to you," said Sir Stephen Compton with a wave of the hand.

Monteiro returned the profound bow made him by the officer.

" Ha !" said the Count, whose English was not very good, " Monsieur di Monteiro, we have heard of you. My goot friend Sir Stephen of you speak often. Brave sailor ! but how come you, a Spaniard, to have a suit to our King ?"

"I consider myself English, as I shall explain to His Majesty, Count, and my great desire to serve in His Majesty's English army."

" Hey, would not the navy suit you better, sir ?"

" As it seems best to His Majesty," returned Monteiro, too anxious to care for talking ; and the conversation proceeded in German between Sir Stephen and the Count.

Presently a bell rang. A door opposite to that by which they entered opened, and

Craggs came forth.   He, too, stopped to
speak to Sir Stephen, and, recognising Monteiro, bowed to him.

"What is that picturesque Spaniard doing
here?" asked Craggs.

"He is going, with my help, to reinstate
the heiress of Langdale in her rights."

"Then I bid him God speed.   Fair Mistress Langley is a charming creature."

"His Majesty will receive Sir Stephen
Compton and Don Juan di Monteiro," said a
splendidly dressed gentleman, coming from
the King's private room.

Sir Stephen stepped forward, followed by
Monteiro, who all this time held a small flat
parcel wrapped in an embroidered silk covering in his left hand.

Their conductor, who was a gentleman-in-
waiting, closed the door behind them, and
they stood before George I.

The salon into which they were ushered
was large and handsome.   The walls hung
with portraits, amongst which Monteiro recognised Henry VII. and his bluff son; Henry,
Prince of Wales, son of James I.; William

III.; Queen Anne; and, over the mantelpiece, the picture of a beautiful woman which he did not recognise : it was that of the Electress Sophia, mother of the King, and not unlike him as he stood beneath it with his back to the fire.

Yet the features of the first George were strongly marked and heavy, the brow retreating, the eyes prominent, the mouth full and somewhat coarse, and the fat which loaded his chin made more remarkable by a tight cravat. The expression of the pale but not sickly-looking face was rather benevolent and not untinged by sensuality.

He was very plainly dressed in a snuff-coloured suit, unadorned by lace or any other ornament, save the broad blue ribbon of the Garter across his chest. He wore a well-powdered wig, flowing in large ringlets on his shoulders, and looked infinitely less kingly than my Lord Sunderland, who stood a little apart to the right, and even less imposing than Parker, the Lord Chancellor, with whom he was conversing.

" Come here, Sir Stephen," said His Majesty

good-humouredly, in French (not very fluent French). " So this is your buccaneering friend ?"

Sir Stephen bowed low. " Now very desirous to be your Majesty's true and faithful servant, if you will permit him. Allow me to present Mr. Rupert Langley, one of the Langdale family."

" He looks more like a Spaniard than an Englishman," returned the King. " Nevertheless, sir, we are willing to accept you as a loyal subject ;" at which gracious speech, and a look from Sir Stephen, Monteiro or, as he must henceforth be called, Rupert Langley, bent his knee and kissed the King's hand. " Now I recall it," resumed His Majesty ; " the Langleys are not specially loyal !—at least not all—your brother or your cousin was expatriated, was he not ?"

" He was, your Majesty, and suffered much in consequence of his unsound judgment. Had opportunity been granted him he would, I am convinced, have proved the sincerity of his conversion ; but that opportunity he missed through the loss of a pardon granted

by her late gracious Majesty," replied
Rupert.

Instead of a rejoinder, the King addressed
himself in German to Sir Stephen Compton,
who replied with a smiling aspect, as though
well pleased, in the same language.

" How is it that you are so sure this pardon
was granted ?" asked the King, turning again
to Rupert Langley.

" Because, sire, I hold it in my hand; and I
have craved the favour of obtaining access to
your presence, that I might place it in your
own royal hand, and implore the restoration
of the lands and title of Langdale to the
orphan daughter of the late lord, now a
penniless dependent on the charity of her
relatives."

So saying, Rupert disengaged the parchment from its covering and, bowing low, presented it to the King, who took and examined
it curiously. It was not long, written in Latin,
and surmounted by a number of flourishes
almost artistic in their complications, while a
huge green seal of soft-looking wax depended
from the document by a strip of parchment.

" ' 'Tis the great seal," said Lord Sunderland, who had approached at a motion from the King.

" See !" said His Majesty to the Lord Chancellor, " it is the signature of Bolingbroke."

" It is, I believe, sire," replied that functionary, looking keenly at the writing ; whereupon the King, turning to Sir Stephen, spoke rapidly and emphatically in German. Indeed, during the whole interview His Majesty did not speak a word of English.

After a rather lengthy reply, Sir Stephen Compton addressed Rupert :

" His Majesty is disposed to accept this document as genuine ;" then, looking to the two Ministers, added : " He desires me to repeat to you the story of its discovery," and proceeded to give the details he had already received from Rupert.

After some questioning on this score, in which the King took part, he said in French to Rupert :

" How is it, sir, that you, who profess so much readiness to enter our service, have been so lately engaged in a conspiracy against us ?

Scarce three years since—was it not, my
lord?" (to Sunderland)—"that an attempt
was made to stir up the peasantry somewhere
in the South, and you tell me this gentleman
and his father were concerned in it. It was
discovered and frustrated, if I remember
right, by another member of this Langdale
family?"

"Yes, sire," replied Rupert quickly, "an
active member, who lights fires in order to
extinguish them! Will your Majesty suffer
me to observe, that the action of my father
was prompted by a personal feeling towards
his old commander? It was more of devotion
to England's High Admiral than rebellion
against England's King which actuated him.
He had long been a stranger to his country,
and knew nothing of politics; for myself,
whither he went, there I was bound
to go also, by my duty as a son, and my
fidelity as the follower of a right noble
captain!"

The King smiled graciously. " It is a pity,
sir, your father's loyalty was misdirected."

" It is, sire! Since those days I have lived

in England and judged for myself, and whether your Majesty deigns to accept my services or no, my convictions will never permit me to draw my sword against your authority."

Monteiro, or Rupert, stepped back as he said this, with a profound bow, and then stood at his full height—a noble figure—one hand resting on his sword-hilt, the other dropped to his side ; his head erect, with a bright fearless look in his eyes, as if, in spite of the profound deference good-breeding exacted, he was perfectly unabashed by the Sovereign's presence.

"I feel bound to tell your Majesty," remarked Lord Sunderland, "that if this gentleman be the son of the late Honourable Rupert Langley, formerly of the royal navy, I can furnish some proof of the sincerity of his professions. Among the papers of the conspirators lately seized in connection with the Sheppard affair, there is a letter, signed 'Rupert Langley,' absolutely refusing to share in any attempt to foment disturbance against the present Government of the country.

Moreover, it is evident that they had opened but very little of their scheme to him."

" I earnestly hope your Majesty will look favourably upon my young friend's suit," put in Sir Stephen.

" I will consider, I will consider! Now touching this pardon. It seems evident the daughter of the exiled Baron is now Baroness Langdale, and properly under your care, my Lord Chancellor. You are the legal guardian of minors."

" The young lady herself craves to be delivered from the guardianship of Mr. John Langley, who is anxious to force her into a marriage with his son," said Sir Stephen eagerly.

" There has been a strange romance respecting that young lady and her marriage," said my Lord Sunderland, and immediately plunged into the oft-told tale, to which the King listened with much interest, occasionally uttering an exclamation in German.

" This is a wondrous history, and a fitting climax to the whole," said His Majesty, when the Earl ceased speaking.

" Pardon me, sire! the climax has yet to be revealed : behold the bridegroom!" and Sir Stephen indicated Rupert Langley by a wave of the hand.

"What!" cried the King. "*This* young gallant? My Lord Chancellor, you must look to your authority! here are the reins seized from your hands before you can grasp them!"

" Permit me, sire, to explain," said Rupert, again stepping forward. After setting forth that it was by means of this stratagem only he could save his kinswoman from what he felt certain would be a miserable destiny, he continued : " I beg your Majesty, and you, my lords, to believe that I hold my cousin in no way bound to me. I have kept the mystery unsolved, as a defence against the schemes of Mr. John Langley. If the young lady is, by your Majesty's gracious permission, placed under the protection of my lord the Chancellor, it only remains for me solemnly to declare her free!"

" Will the demoiselle thank you for your freedom?" said the King, who seemed in a marvellously amiable mood. "I imagine she will not be ready to renounce a gallant cavalier who has done her such service!"

"Sire, that remains to be proved!"

"Where is the young lady at present?" asked the Chancellor.

"Under the care of her aunt, the Countess of Helmsford," replied Sir Stephen; "but that lady sets out for Paris to-morrow or next day, and it is proposed that Mistress Langley —perhaps I should say the Baroness Langdale—should take up her abode with me and my daughter."

This arrangement found favour with the legal custodian of infants. After an animated conversation in German with Sir Stephen Compton, and some discussion in French with Sunderland, the King gave Sir Stephen his hand to kiss, as though dismissing them.

"You have His Majesty's permission to remove your kinswoman to my care," said the Baronet; "also to consider yourself attached to his service; in what capacity you shall learn hereafter."

Monteiro bowed low and, after a few words

of thanks, followed Sir Stephen from the royal presence.

"I congratulate you, my young friend, on your entire success!" cried that gentleman, as they stood waiting for the carriage to draw up. "I have seldom known His Majesty so gracious or so talkative as this morning! Your story has interested him greatly!"

"You have been my good genius, Sir Stephen!" cried Rupert. "Complete your benefits by accompanying me to St. James's Square. I burn to announce the good news! and the sooner my young cousin is removed to your hospitable mansion the better."

"I am completely at your service," said the polite Baronet.

The short distance was accomplished in silence on Rupert Langley's side, although Sir Stephen Compton talked amply—of his influence with the King, of the tremendous blow the whole affair would be to John Langley; but Rupert's heart was full. He was at the crisis of his fate—a few minutes more and he would stand in Maud's presence and—Lady Helmsford's.

It seemed a lifetime, that short transit ; but it was past.

The coach stopped at Lady Helmsford's door.

The first glance at the unswept door-steps, the roadway much trampled and furrowed by wheels, startled and chilled Rupert. He sprang to the ground before the gorgeous footman could disentangle himself from his fellows on the foot-board, and sounded the knocker with a will.

Two, three minutes, a century passed.

" Is the house shut up ?" called Sir Stephen from the coach.

As he spoke, Rupert heard the sounds of bolts being withdrawn and chains unhooked. Then the door was opened a few inches, and the porter's face presented itself.

" What is the matter ? Is my lady within ?" cried Monteiro eagerly.

" Bless your heart ! no, sir ; she started about ten this morning for Dover," replied the man, opening the portal to its full extent, now he recognised his interrogator.

" At ten this morning ?" repeated Rupert,

struck with a sudden sense of treachery and evil-doing.

"What is it ?" asked Sir Stephen, joining him.

"Lady Helmsford has already set out on her journey," replied Rupert. " But Mistress Langley," he continued to the porter; "is she not within ?"

" No, sir, no ! Mistress Langley started yesterday, between two and three o'clock, under charge of Mistress Sparrow, so as to precede her ladyship by a stage or two. They were to lie last night at Rochester." So he had heard her ladyship's new secretary say.

Rupert was struck dumb for a moment. "And Mistress Langley's woman Dorothy—did she go with her lady?"

That the man did not know. Mistress Dorothy had gone out in the forenoon yesterday, and he had not seen her since.

" Not seen her since !" repeated Rupert to himself, thinking, with a flash of bitter self-contempt, of the satisfaction he had derived from D'Arcy's report of this out-going of

Dorothy's on the previous day! Now it seemed to him but part of some infernal scheme to blind and bamboozle him.

" Then you are alone in the house ?" he said aloud.

" No, your honour. Master Hobson, the butler, and his wife are left as care-takers. He is just gone forth, and charged me to keep the door barred and bolted."

" You are quite sure Mistress Langley was to travel in Mistress Sparrow's company, in advance of Lady Helmsford ?" reiterated Rupert.

" So I heard them all say, sir."

" This is a very strange tale," said Sir Stephen Compton aside. " What induces the Countess to spirit off her niece thus ? I have heard queer tales of my lady. Have you made love to the aunt, Monteiro, or Langley ? and is jealousy of a younger rival the motive power, you scapegrace ?"

" It is too serious for jesting," said Rupert sternly. " We must lose no time in overtaking the travellers. I am certain Maud has been forced away against her will !"

" But they have good four hours' start !"

cried the Baronet. " They must be at Rochester by this time."

" They are heavily-laden, sir. A horseman
will soon come up with them. I must not ask
you to join me in this chase," continued
Rupert, quivering with eagerness as he
spoke.

" Were it not for rheumatism—" began Sir
Stephen apologetically.

" No, no, of course not," interrupted
Rupert ; " but may I ask you to send a couple
of your servants to back me in the attempt to
rescue my cousin ? Their presence will prove
to her that she will not be indebted to me
only, but that the good and noble Mistress
Compton is ready to receive her."

" I will gladly send my house-steward, who
is quite confidential, and two of the men ; but
where shall they find you ?"

" Oh, I will stay for them at the Tabard.
I have to provide myself with horses and
money, and seek my trusty friend, D'Arcy,
who knows the country round London, which
I do not. If your people will follow to the
Tabard Inn, they will probably be before me.

Let the first comers wait. There is no time to lose! May I implore you to go straight home?"

"I will do so without fail. I wish you God-speed, my young friend. Why do you seem so uneasy? 'Tis an awkward *contretemps!* but no harm can happen to the young lady."

"Heaven knows," said Rupert, a fierce look coming into his eyes; "only God help them that do her the lightest wrong when I come to reckon with them! This movement of Lady Helmsford is past my comprehension; but I will not keep you, Sir Stephen. Here —a coach—some one fetch me a coach!"

"*I* will, your honour," cried a rough, unkempt-looking youth, who had followed Sir Stephen Compton's carriage from St. James's, perhaps in the hope of earning a few pence by helping to hold horses or run an errand, "*I* will!"

They had not noticed him, though he was close behind them on the door-steps.

"Go then—be quick!" exclaimed Rupert.

He turned to assist Sir Stephen into his

carriage again, exhorting him to speed; and
the vehicle had hardly been put in motion,
when the volunteer messenger appeared,
standing on the step of a hackney coach,
which clattered up to where Rupert stood
revolving in his mind the most rapid mode of
action. Robilliard would find him horses, and
there, too, he would probably meet D'Arcy,
who might follow with the steeds to his
lodging, while he made some necessary
change in his dress.

"Drive to Lamb's Court, Holborn, as fast
as you can," he said distinctly to the driver,
bestowing a small gratuity on the errand boy,
who stood an instant pouring forth profuse
thanks, then ran violently after the carriage,
jumped up behind, and rode with it till it
reached Long Acre, when he let himself down
and went swiftly in the direction of Great
Queen Street.

Meantime Rupert Langley strove to steady
his brain and order his thoughts. Perhaps
the most consolatory circumstance in this
curious countermarch of Lady Helmsford's
was that Maud was sent away with Mistress

Letitia Sparrow. From her, he firmly believed, no double dealing was to be feared. Dim possibilities of deeper treachery than the mere inconvenience of Maud's being dragged half way to Dover occurred to him as he rattled, rolled, and bumped through the devious streets which led to Holborn; but to nothing that might seriously injure Maud would the kindly, timid *dame de compagnie* lend herself. Still it was infernally annoying, and he mentally consigned the Countess to very warm quarters for her troublesome freak.

Arrived at "Lambs'," he was at once shown into Robilliard's room, and quickly told his errand.

"What does my lady the Countess mean by carrying off our young Baroness in that fashion? *Mort de ma vie!* a noble lady like her would not be in league with the scoundrels that want to snap her up! Are you *sure* she is with Lady Helmsford?"

"Don't distract me, Robilliard. She is, I am certain, with the Countess's *dame de com-*

pagnie—a good faithful creature; but you will find me horses—stout, fleet, serviceable— I care not what price is put on them. I shall pay all and everything, once I unravel this cursed coil, if I have not a sous left! Where is D'Arcy?"

"He went hence scarce half an hour ago, to go down to your Excellency's lodgings, and hear what news you had."

"All was well till I found the young Baroness gone! for she is Baroness—Mistress of the Heritage of Langdale, Robilliard! The King confirms the pardon granted by his predecessor; but I must away, good friend! Send on the horses as fast as you can. No doubt I shall find D'Arcy awaiting me." So saying he returned to his coach, and drove as fast as the capabilities of the cattle would permit to his lodgings.

As he expected, he found D'Arcy passing the time with a pipe and a tankard.

Calling for his valet, Rupert proceeded rapidly to change the suit in which he had appeared at Court, and to draw on high riding-boots, explaining while he did so the necessity for following Lady Helmsford as speedily as possible.

"I count on your help, D'Arcy. Thrust a couple of pistols in your belt, man ; I scarce know what or whom we may encounter."

While he spoke, Rupert unlocked the cabinet where he kept those weapons, and bestowed a brace on his follower, setting him an example by placing another in the sash or belt he had girt over his riding-coat, attaching them to silk cords which he passed round his neck, buccaneer fashion, to avoid losing them in a *mêlée.*

" Faith !" cried D'Arcy, as he looked to the priming of the weapons just received, "it is an ugly business. I don't like the looks of it at all. I wonder what they have done with Dorothy ; the poor soul will be combing their hair for them if they keep her from her lady."

" I trust she is with the young Baroness by this time," said Rupert, who was filling his purse with all the coin left in a certain small inner drawer of the same cabinet. "I do not imagine Lady Helmsford would separate

them. Dorothy was probably only sent on in
advance."

"God knows !" replied D'Arcy, with a shake
of the head. " Her ladyship the Countess
wouldn't hand her over to that black devil,
John Langley, now ?"

"No, no! Furious as she is, I think her
incapable of such villainy ; besides, I have her
own written assurance that John Langley had
made no move. No; she would not voluntarily send back her niece to that traitor."

"Well, you know best, sir."

"I wish the horses were here!" cried
Rupert; "'tis near three o'clock. We can
scarce overtake them before nightfall, which
will increase our difficulties tenfold."

"The horses are at the door, monsieur,"
said Victor.

"Good ; come along, D'Arcy."

The horses sent by Robilliard were far
above the average, both in speed and strength;
and, after exchanging a few words of commen-
dation, Rupert Langley and his follower rode
on almost in unbroken silence till they reached
London Bridge.

"The Tabard is near the other end of the Bridge?" asked Rupert. "I have never visited it save once."

"It is! 'Tis scarce five minutes' ride beyond."

The next moment they were passing between the curious ancient buildings that encumbered the Bridge, at this hour crowded with vehicles and passengers, for the passage was not wide enough for the traffic. The two horsemen made their way but slowly, Rupert's thoughts too busily and uneasily engaged to allow of his bestowing attention on the picturesqueness of the structure, nor that strange edifice, Nonsuch House.

At last they penetrated to the embattled gate tower on the Southwark side: here they were again stopped by the passage of a huge waggon, Rupert chafing and tearing his heart with all kinds of conjectures (none of them pleasant). At last they were clear of the Bridge, and, leaving the square towers of the fine old church, St. Mary Overy, on the right, they rode at a quick pace into the yard of the famous Tabard Inn.

It was surrounded on three sides by the house itself, round the second story of which ran a heavy wooden gallery, supported by stout wooden posts or pillars. Beneath them were benches for visitors to rest upon, while on the left side was a pump and trough, for the refreshment of their cattle.

Rupert glanced round. A post-chaise without horses stood in one corner, a waggoner was watering his beasts at the trough; but there was no sign of Sir Stephen Compton's servants.

" No ; I will not dismount," said Rupert to the ostler and tapster, who ran out to wait upon him. " I expect three more of my company to join us here ; then we will have a cup of ale, and press on. Tell me," he continued, as a sudden thought struck him, " did Lady Helmsford pause here, in passing on her journey to the coast this morning, about three or four hours ago? A lady travelling in some state, with two carriages ?"

" No, your honour. Such a party passed, but did not stop."

" No," put in the ostler ; " but yester-even

a coach-and-four paused here for a while ; one of the horses had gone suddenly lame, and they were forced to take another."

" And who were in the coach ?" asked Rupert eagerly. " Any ladies ?"

" Ay, one or two, I know ! for a little dog broke away from them, and one of the ladies was in sore fear lest it should be lost."

" Was one of the ladies young ?"

" I am not sure there were two on 'em ; 'twas t'other ostler attended that coach. I were a-looking arter one that had just come in from Canterbury."

" And where is the other ostler ? Bring him to me at once."

" Here, Bill ! Why, Bill, where be ye ?" And ostler number one clattered across the yard in search of the other ; but he was nowhere to be found. At last a nondescript hanger-on of the establishment remembered that " Missis had sent him somewheres."

While the search was going on the three expected horsemen rode into the yard. The leader, a grave, well-dressed personage, lifting his hat, presented a note to Rupert. It contained a few lines from Sir Stephen Compton, to identify his servants, and place them at Rupert's disposal.

"You see your master's wishes," said he, handing the note to the bearer to peruse. "What is your name?"

"Hammond, sir, at your service."

Having paid for the refreshment he had ordered, Rupert and his party looked to their girths, to their horses' shoes, to their own arms, and then rode as briskly down the High Street of Southwark as heaps of offal and rubbish, loose stones and deep ruts would permit.

Rupert looked at his watch — twenty minutes to four. How fast time flew! How fast his heart beat as he thought of the doubtful end which awaited his ride.

What if Maud, turned against him by the representations or misrepresentations of her aunt, refused to return with him, what power had he to compel her? He would only have the melancholy consolation of knowing that she was safe and a free agent. He wished he had asked the Chancellor for some authority — something to back his own word.

If, on the contrary, Maud had been forced out of London (and some inner voice seemed to tell him she had), what a delicious necessity would arise of her trusting herself to him !

The approach of night would no doubt increase her reluctance to accept his protection; but, with Dorothy to bear her company, all might be arranged to spare the object of his deepest, tenderest solicitude the smallest annoyance.

If Dorothy was not with her mistress, then no doubt Maud was being treated as a prisoner; and perhaps, feeling that he was her only true disinterested friend, she might turn to him in her hour of need, and accept the relationship in which they stood to each other.

This was too delicious a thought. The effort to resist it made Rupert strike his spurs into his steed ; but the next instant he checked his career, as two men and four horses turned the corner of a side road, and met him face to face.

By this time the houses at either side the street had grown more straggling and farther apart; they had nearly cleared the suburbs.

Directly Rupert saw the men just mentioned, he recognised them to be post-boys; and, although coming from the direction they did was not encouraging, he thought he would ask them whence they came.

"We have come across from Streatham," replied the man he spoke to, "and are going to the Tabard Inn, to return this 'ere brown horse, as we was forced to borrow last evening."

"Ha!" cried Rupert; "then you conveyed some of Lady Helmsford's party the first stage of their journey?"

"We did, your honour!" cried the second and younger post-boy, pressing forward; "and one of the ladies charged me with a message, because she could find no way to write."

"What was it?" cried Rupert, all eagerness.

"Nay, I won't tell save to him it was meant for," said the man resolutely.

"Was it an old or a young lady charged you with it ?"

" Oh, it was th' ould one ; and I would have gone straight this morning, only a gentleman came up to the inn at ——, wanting horses on to his house at Streatham, so we have just come from thence."

" Tell me," cried Rupert, with a sudden inspiration, " was the message to be carried to Don Juan di Monteiro, in Salisbury Street, Strand ?"

" It was, sir," replied the man in much surprise.

" I am he ! Speak."

" I scarce know what to do ; but you look like a true man, sir. And the lady said you would give me half-a-crown."

" Here it is," said Rupert, drawing forth the coin, " ready for you when you have spoken."

" Well, sir, she said, ' Tell the gentleman that the young lady has been given up to Master John Langley ; and that she earnestly prays Don Monteiro to help her.' "

" Then where did you part with the young lady ? or did she start with you ?"

" She did, sir; and we stopped in Great Queen Street to set her down and her boxes."

" By Heaven, D'Arcy, your suggestion is too true !" cried Rupert. " One word more. Did an elderly woman — a waiting-woman —descend with the young lady ?"

" No, sir ; none but herself, and I think it warn't all comfortable like. T'other lady cried, and had hard work to come at speech with me."

" There's your half-crown for you, my man, and there's another on my own account. Come, D'Arcy ! we have to make up for lost time ! Who could have believed a woman would lay so deep a plot to betray another !"

" Faith, it's just what I would believe !" ejaculated D'Arcy. " Where to now, Excellency ?" For Rupert had wheeled his horse round quickly.

" To Great Queen Street ; to that villain's house ! Hammond, I have certain tidings of

the young lady we seek, and we must turn
our horses' heads in an opposite direction.
Follow, all, as fast as may be, to Great Queen
Street, if you lose sight of me ; but keep up
as well as you can."

So saying, Rupert set spurs to his horse
and rode as rapidly as the various impedi-
ments offered by the Bridge and streets would
permit.

" And what's your plan now, sir ?" asked
D'Arcy, who managed to come up alongside
him.

" I have none," exclaimed Rupert, " except
to force my way into the ruffian's house and
search it from garret to cellar, if we do so at
the sword's point ! God grant we may find
Mistress Maud there !"

" Amen," said D'Arcy. " But it's a
chance."

Rupert did not reply ; he felt he dared not
think of the horrible ills that might befall—
nay, might have befallen his beloved ! He
urged on his horse, in a whirl of fevered anti-
cipation, the wildest visions of vengeance
firing his brain. D'Arcy kept near him, but

the others were soon distanced.   At last they reached their goal.

Rupert, glancing down the street, saw that something unusual had occurred.

A small crowd was gathered round a mansion, half-way down.   Ragged boys had perched themselves on the railing, and were pointing and jeering at some object apparently on the door-step.   "Oh! look at the mad Frenchwoman."

"She's a witch!   Let's take her and duck her in Rosamond's Pool!   Call the beadle, and he'll soon put her in jail for a vagrant!"

"Make way there," cried Rupert, laying about him smartly with his whip, as these and similar sentences caught his ear.

The crowd opened right and left instantly, for a well-dressed imperious gentleman; and Rupert saw, with unspeakable dismay, Dorothy seated on the door-step.   Her hood had fallen back, dragging her cap with it; her grey locks dishevelled, her face covered by her hands, and her whole attitude expressive of utter, absolute despair.

"Dorothy!" cried Rupert, springing to the

ground, while D'Arcy caught his rein. " Dorothy, what — what has happened ? Where is your mistress ?"

" Is it yourself, Master Monteiro ?" she cried, starting to her feet and grasping his hand in both her own. " Oh ! where have you been, to let her be taken away, and me not knowing what's become of her ? Sure, I've been shut up like a maniac, till I'm almost driven mad in earnest ; and they laugh at me here, and slap the door in mee face. I can get no word of her !"

" I will make them open !" cried Rupert. " Stand back there," he called to the crowd, " or my men who are coming up will ride over you !"

The people immediately obeyed, and Rupert proceeded to thunder at the door.

It was quickly opened by Langley's sedate, imperturbable *major domo*.

" I seek Mistress Maud Langley," said Rupert, instantly stepping on the threshold.

" She is not here, sir," was the calmly civil reply.

" Where is she gone, then ?"

" She started on her journey to Langdale Priory this morning."

" Are you lying ?" asked Rupert sternly.

" 'Tis true, sir.   You may enter and search the house; and indeed some of these onlookers may have seen the party start, for there are always idlers about !"

" Did Master Langley accompany the young lady ?"

" No, sir !   Master Langley had been summoned to meet my Lord Berkeley out Roehampton way ; but my wife attended the young lady."

Rupert thought a moment ; then, seizing the man by the collar, with a sudden powerful effort, dragged him down the steps within reach of D'Arcy.

" Hold him," he said ; and D'Arcy laid a strong grasp on the astonished butler, thus making sure the door should not be closed.

" Tell me," said Rupert, seizing a boy from the front rank of the spectators, " what time did a travelling party leave this house to-day ?

or did you see one ? Speak truth ! I will not hurt you !"

" No, sir," blubbered the youth thus addressed ; " I saw never a one. I only come in the street half an hour ago !"

" But *I* was here, and saw the coach-and-four drive off !" called out a smaller boy shrilly.

" Ha !" exclaimed Rupert; " tell me what you did see ?"

" First the coach drew up, and two men a 'ossback beside it ; and then another man gets up on the box, and they ties on some big leather packages ; and then a mighty dark gentleman leads out a beautiful young lady, and puts her and an elderly, cross-looking woman in the coach, and they drives off !"

" What time of the day was this ?" asked Rupert sharply.

" I heard the church clocks strike two a little before," said the boy.

" One word more," exclaimed Rupert, turning to D'Arcy's prisoner, " and you shall be set free ! Where is Captain Harold Langley ?"

" I know not, sir," replied the man sullenly.
"He left here three or four days ago. I know
not whither he went."

" Release him," said Rupert.

" Thank you, sir," said the man, who had
not made the slightest resistance. " My
master will reckon with you for the usage you
have bestowed upon his servant."

" When your master has reckoned with
me he will not be in the mood to settle many
other scores !" said Rupert sternly.

" Oh, ye black-faced designing devil !"
screamed Dorothy ; " you are like your
master ! If a hair of my darling's head is
hurt, I'll tear him limb from limb !"

" You shall," returned Rupert ; " but for
the present control yourself. D'Arcy ! this
story of a journey to Langdale is a blind ! Had
they started by the right road at two or
shortly after, we should have overtaken
them ! It is but an infernal scheme to entrap
Maud, and carry her to the lonely house you
have reconnoitred ! You shall guide us there ;
I feel certain we shall run the villains to earth !
Come, Dorothy ! pull yourself together, my

woman! You shall accompany us to cheer your fair mistress!"

After a short consultation with Hammond, it was determined that the elder of Sir Stephen's two servants should find Mistress Dorothy a coach with a tolerable pair of horses, and bring her after them as quickly as might be.

" Follow the Uxbridge Road till you pass the toll-bar at Shepherd's Bush," said D'Arcy; " then strike away up a lane on the right— 'twill bring you to a sort of common—and then past a wide pool and clump of trees. You will see the house, and find something of a fray, or I'm much mistaken."

" Lose no time!" cried Rupert. " Remember, my good fellow, you shall be well rewarded for this day's work."

So saying, Rupert and the rest rode off at speed—away down Holborn and on to the Uxbridge Road—soon leaving traffic and houses behind them.

Often in his dreams, when disturbed or unwell, in after years, did the agonies of that ride—the fears that would not be silenced, the fevered impatience, the intolerable slowness of the quickest pace to which he could urge his horse—return to Rupert Langley.

It was an age of endurance, an hour burnt into his memory for ever.

CHAPTER VIII.

HAROLD LANGLEY was exceedingly puzzled to answer the question with which the last chapter but one closed, and so met it by another.

"I hope you have not been frightened! that you do not mistake the motives which prompt me to arrest your progress! Will you please descend, fair cousin?"

"No, Harold, I do not please to descend! I wish to continue my journey according to your father's directions! Is it possible you dare to interfere with them?"

"Oh, sir!" cried Mistress Mathews; "what is the meaning of this? Master Langley charged me to take the utmost care of the young lady, and give her safe into the hands of her own woman, who awaits her at the Ferry! Indeed, sir, you should not ruin a poor creature's chances of employment by your pranks!"

"Come, none of this nonsense!" cried Harold coarsely. "Here, Strange, pull this woman out of the coach! and keep her away till I induce my lady to hear reason! If she won't, why we must only use other means!"

Upon this the man called Strange—a great, broad-shouldered, jovial-looking bully —stepped to the carriage and pulled forth Mistress Mathews very unceremoniously, she screaming and striking at him the while. She was hustled away round a corner of the house, Maud being almost speechless with terror and indignation at this display of brutal force. What was to become of her? Would to Heaven she was back with her guardian— there at least she would be safe from Harold!

"Your new waiting-woman shows as much fight as the old one would have done! Let her scream away," he added, removing his mask with a triumphant laugh. " There is no one to listen—no need for disguise at *my* country seat ! It's such a nice quiet spot, I thought it would be well for you to rest on your journey, and hear me plead my own cause, as you never would when we were in company. Come, sweet lady ! will you deign to alight ? or shall I have the happiness of lifting you out in my arms ?"

Something—she could not define what—in Harold's tone turned Maud cold and sick with apprehension.

" I will descend !" she cried. " Do not attempt to touch me !"

Harold laughed unpleasantly, and stepped back, to permit of her leaving the carriage.

As soon as her foot touched the ground, she paused and looked deliberately right and left.

Before the melancholy, dilapidated house was a wide stretch of marshy common, with a distant rising ground to the right. A road, little more than a cart-track, led past a broken fence, interlaced with furze-bushes, which

marked the boundary of the place. A little
farther, in the direction of the high ground,
was a wide, dark, sullen pool, which the level
rays of the fast-sinking sun failed to touch;
and beyond that a scattered clump of ragged
pollard elms. Nothing could surpass the loneliness and desolation of the scene. The figures
grouped round (three or four masked men on
horseback); the riderless steed of the ruffian
who had dealt so summarily with Maud's
companion, cropping the grass; the dismounted postillions, rubbing down and attend-
ing to their blown horses, were all of life
within the wide range of sight, and they were
all in Harold's service !

Never before did Maud's heart so utterly
despair. Mistress Mathews' cries had ceased.

"Harold !" cried Maud, shivering at the
awful silence; "for Heaven's sake, see that
the poor woman be not hurt ! do not let them
hurt her !"

"Zounds, no ! None will harm her ! So
soon as the horses have breathed, she shall be
driven back in state to the place from whence
she came."

" Do not send her away !" urged Maud, her mouth feeling almost too dry to form the sounds. " Though she is a stranger, she is better than none. I prefer her to any one you can have found to wait upon me."

" I will be your lady's-maid myself," returned Harold, with another unpleasant laugh. " But come, fairest mistress ! 'tis no use reconnoitring the premises ; come indoors !"

" Is it possible," cried Maud, " that you dare to act thus, without your father's knowledge ?"

" Fathers have flinty hearts, and are too cold and slow to satisfy a lover's impatience !" said Harold affectedly.

Maud suddenly darted to the nearest postillion.

" If you are a true Englishman," she said rapidly, " make your way to Don Juan di Monteiro—to Salisbury Street ! Tell him where I am ! He will amply reward you !"

" Come !" cried Harold, seizing her rudely by the wrist. " That is a bold stroke, but it will not do. Even if the fellow ventured to give your message, the cursed Spaniard is twenty miles off on the Dover Road by this time, in chase of my Lady Helmsford! Our —I mean my emissary saw him safe off on the wrong track before *you* started. Come in, I tell you! There is no help for you. You should not compel me to be rough! I am in truth your devoted slave!"

"Do not touch me!" repeated Maud, shrinking from him. "I will enter the house without resistance, as it is vain; but mark me, Harold, when your father comes to reckon with you, I will not intercede for you, nor seek to save you from the punishment you so richly deserve!"

So saying, she walked straight into the house, followed closely by Harold, who only replied to her last words by saying, "It's a bargain."

The hall of the old mansion was of fair proportions, and the oaken floor, though sorely in need of soap and house-flannel, was in good preservation. The plaster, however, had fallen in many places, both from the walls and the ceiling; and the darkness of the staircase, and deserted aspect of the entrance, seemed to Maud in ominous keeping with her own anticipations. An open door on the left hand showed her a large, scantily-furnished room, with the remains of a roughly-spread meal upon the table, and a good fire in a wide fireplace.

"Your rooms are above," said Captain Langley. "I must trouble you to ascend."

"I prefer remaining here," replied Maud, pausing by the open door.

"I am extremely sorry to coerce you," rejoined Harold with a grin; "but if you will not walk upstairs, mine must be the delightful task of carrying you!"

Maud silently ascended, stopping when she reached the wide landing, off which a couple of doors and as many long dark passages opened.

"Allow me," said Harold, passing her, and unfastening one of the doors. He motioned to his prisoner to enter.

The room into which she was ushered was of good size, panelled with oak, made cheerful by a good fire, and lit by two tall narrow windows opposite the door. At the end of the room, to the left, was a recess that looked as if it ought to be a bay-window, but was panelled like the rest of the room. A square of faded carpet was spread before the fire, where was an arm-chair and two others ; a worked foot-stool, the pattern much obliterated ; and a queer, foreign-looking table with many legs. Evidently some attempt had been made to render the apartment habitable.

"Pray sit down by the fire, fair cousin, and let us have a talk. Will you not remove your hat and scarf? Though 'tis but a poor place, I should like to see you seem at home in *my* house. By-and-by, Maud, we shall have a grander dwelling !"

"Harold," she said, "once more, why have you brought me here ?"

"To make you my wedded wife, till death us do part," he replied, seating himself opposite to her, and laying his hat and mask on the floor.

"But you know that is impossible. I *cannot* wed any one till the Langdale marriage is dissolved ; nor will I, Harold ! You may kill me, but you cannot force my lips to say 'yes.'"

" Well, we will see !" returned Harold, with a poor assumption of bravado. " How is it that you do not fancy me for a husband, cousin ? I am sure I have sought you perseveringly ! I am gone to a shadow for love of you, and now I have dared even my father's anger to secure you. Indeed, adorable cousin, if you were just a little kind, I would be your devoted slave !"

Here the sound of horses trampling and the rolling of a heavy carriage fell on Maud's ear.

" Harold !" she cried, starting from her seat and rushing to the window ; " is that the coach driving away with Mistress Mathews ?"

" I imagine it is," he replied.

" You surely have some woman here to keep me company !" exclaimed Maud, horror-struck at being left alone in the hands of such a set of ruffians as Harold's *employés* appeared to be.

The look-out from the window was melancholy and unpromising : a filthy, ragged, empty farm-yard ; a half-ruined stable, through the open door of which she could see some horses feeding; and beyond, the silent, lonely common.

"You are enough to have on one's hands, without any more of your charming sex," said he, with an awkward attempt at jocularity.

"Listen, Harold!" cried Maud, almost beside herself with sickening terror, yet striving gallantly to preserve her self-control; "I believe I am at this moment Baroness Langdale. I firmly believe that before many days are over I shall be in possession of my lands. I shall be rich, and you, my cousin, need money! you are in debt, or you would never want to marry *me!* Take me back to your father—to Lady Helmsford's house—to Lord Chedworth—to any one—and I will pay your debts! I will give you half my fortune!"

Harold listened with a strong inclination to come to terms. He was neither nice nor sensitive, but he did not like the task his father had set him. He was not strong enough either to love or hate intensely, and to do anything disagreeable was intolerable to him.

"You may trust me, Harold," she resumed, seeing that he hesitated. "I would not break my word!"

"Ay, most generous kinswoman!" he said, laughing, as he collected his thoughts, and saw the uselessness of the proposition ; "but you will be a minor for nearly two years longer ; besides, you forget I am in love with you!" and he seized her hand. "So nothing short of——"

A sudden heavy knock startled him. He let go the hand Maud was struggling to withdraw, and opened the door a few inches. A short colloquy in gruff whispers ensued, and then Harold, turning to her, said :

"Pray forgive me for my discourtesy! I am compelled to leave you for a while ;" and immediately left the room, turning the key, however, audibly as he did so.

Left alone, Maud relaxed the strain of her self-control and yielded to an agony of tears, which somewhat relieved her.

Then she surveyed her prison. The recess, she found, was a bay-window, closely shut-

tered, and too securely fastened for her to
open. The other windows seemed to be in
the side of the mansion, nor could her efforts
open them.

She observed the fading light. Was it
possible that she was beyond the reach of
help ? The glass, set in leaden lattice-work,
seemed thick and strong. A sound or cry
could scarce penetrate it.

What should she do ? She looked round
despairingly ; her eye was caught by the fire-
irons—a poker and pair of tongs. She seized
the former, and, with as little noise as she
could make, broke several of the small panes
of glass, so that she might call to any possible
passer-by.

Then, with fear and trembling, she pushed
open a door on the right of the fireplace. It
led into a large bedroom, scantily furnished
—one window completely stopped up and
another partially. A gloomy, repellent
chamber, with a small, mysterious-looking
door in the panelling at the farther side
of the bed—a room into which Maud resolved
not again to enter. She returned to the

fireside, and, sitting down by the table, rested her arms upon it, covering her face with her hands, and, after an earnest prayer for help, abandoned herself to a painful broken succession of memories and antici- pations.

Meantime, Harold had obeyed a summons from his father, and found him in the room below, where he was impatiently awaiting the saddling of another horse, his own having cast a shoe.

" 'Tis the only check we have had," he ob- served. " Even now, if those unhandy knaves would but hasten, I would have time enough to gallop back to the Horse-ferry, mount the steed I left there, and reach my Lord Berke- ley in time! None could then for a moment suspect my complicity in this plot. How does our captive seem ?"

" Less outrageous than I expected, but very deadly and resolute. She offered to pay my debts and divide her fortune with me if I would take her safe back to *you.* Ha ! ha ! ha ! 'twas a tempting offer."

"Fool!" muttered John Langley. "Harold, you will never be worthy of me! Now I have put fortune once more within your grasp. I have done all the work, and done it well."

"You have indeed, sir! What did you do with that witch Dorothy?"

"Oh, she went to prepare her mistress's lodgings in Bow Street, in the house of a worthy couple who are a little behind with their rent. They turned the key on her by mistake; and were not to unlock the door till past three to-day. I dare say she is now roaming the streets, finding her bird flown, if she is not already taken up as a madwoman."

"The Countess proved our best friend after all."

"Ay, Harold! she surpasses us in scheming by a good deal; but it was a narrow chance our securing the heiress."

After a little more talk, and arranging how John Langley's search for the fugitives was to seem eager and yet be misdirected, he exclaimed:

"I will go forth myself, and mount at the

back of the house. I marvel what keeps
them; why, it is more than six o'clock!
Farewell, Harold! The game is in your own
hands; see that you play it out boldly and
relentlessly !"

He turned to go, when Harold exclaimed
eagerly, " Listen !"

Langley paused, his hand on the lock.

"'Tis but the wind," he said.

" It is the tramp of more horses than one,"
cried Harold uneasily.

" You are nervous," said his father with a
sneer. " 'Tis but some stray gentlemen of
the road."

" Our men are safe out of sight ?" asked
Harold.

" Ay, they are in the kitchen at the back ;
there is nothing to attract attention to this
deserted-looking place. They will be past
directly."

The sounds grew nearer and more distinct.
Father and son stood perfectly still, and the
next moment a long piercing cry from somewhere over their heads rang out through the
still evening air :

"Help! help! for God's sake, help!"

"How has she contrived to open the windows? Run, Harold; stop her!"

But Harold was already halfway upstairs; and, even while he went, the sound of footsteps approaching, a loud knocking at the door, a shout of "Open, in the King's name!" put John Langley on his mettle, and roused his inventive mind to a last effort.

The door remaining closed, the sounds of several feet trampling rapidly round the end of the house, warned him that the new comers were seeking another mode of ingress. He dropped his mask, threw off his cloak, and stood back behind the door.

Maud had sat for some time in a state of semi-stupefaction, till the first distant sound of horses' feet struck her ear and startled her into intense eager life and watchfulness. She darted to the window, and pressed her little ear against the broken panes. Yes! some one—more than one—rode towards her prison-house. Some deliverers sent by God! She waited yet a moment; and then, with all the force she could muster, sent forth the long wailing shriek which had alarmed her jailers.

She had just repeated it, when Harold burst into the room, dragged her from the window, and would no doubt have stifled her cries had his right arm not been useless.

" Hush, or it will be worse for you ! By ——, you'll force me to silence you for ever ! What do you want, you wild cat ?"

Undeterred by his threats, Maud struggled to reach the door, calling as loud as she could for assistance, while sounds of oaths and the clash of steel, a heavy fall, a rush of feet, came up from below. All passed quicker than it can be written ; then the door was flung violently open, and Rupert Langley, followed by D'Arcy and two others, crowded into the room.

At sight of him, Maud stretched out her arms and made an attempt to dart towards him ; but Harold himself was between them.

" Insolent adventurer !" he cried, " how dare you intrude yourself into my house ?"

" Base schemer ! how dare *you* molest and imprison the Baroness Langdale ? Stand back ! I defer your punishment until I have delivered the lady from your vile hands."

He sprang upon Harold as he spoke ; but as he touched him, John Langley, followed by two or three men, came quickly out of the inner room, to Maud's terror and astonishment.

"Stop !" he exclaimed in a voice so hard and collected that all paused to listen.

Maud drew behind the great chair, and Rupert's attention was diverted from his foe.

" You, Sir Spaniard, must accept *me* as your antagonist—my son's sword-arm is disabled— that is, unless you hear reason and quit the house. *I* am here to rescue and defend my ward. Some time after she set out on her journey, I accidentally discovered my son's mad and reprehensible scheme to intercept and carry her off. I lost no time in hastening after her ; and was in the act of rebuking my son when you broke rudely in. You are, I suppose, sent by the Countess of Helmsford ; but I shall myself escort the young lady to her house. Now, sir, be wise—go in peace ! I have a larger force than yours, and the power of the law behind me."

"Treacherous dog!" cried Rupert; "I come to deliver her from you as well as from your son. Stand back, or not even her presence shall save your life! I am no Spaniard. Look on me, murderer, and you will see I am the son and avenger of Rupert Langley!" He dashed aside his feathered hat as he spoke; and John Langley recoiled a step or two, yet rallied again quickly.

"Come on!" cried Rupert to his followers, "our business is to remove this lady, if it cost the life of every man opposed to us." He flashed out his sword as he spoke and crossed that of Langley.

"Be warned," cried the latter, "I have the legal right of guardian over this lady. Beware you fall not foul of the law!"

At these words Sir Stephen Compton's servants hesitated visibly, and looked at each other.

"And I have the legal right of a husband to remove her," exclaimed Rupert. "Speak, dear Maud; am I not your husband?"

"You are, you are!" she cried, stretching out her arms to him. "I am his wife, Master Langley, as *you* know, who were present at our wedding. Let me go to my husband" (for Langley had caught her arm as she attempted to rush towards Rupert).

"Dare not to touch her!" he cried, infuriated by this. "Defend yourself!" and he attacked Langley so fiercely, that he was compelled to let Maud go; she immediately flew to D'Arcy, who placed himself before her sword in hand.

"If any gentleman would like a little practice, I should be happy to oblige him," he said, blandly addressing the men who, with Harold, stood astonished hearers of the altercation.

The Compton servants, too, completely reassured by this sudden revelation, pressed forward.

"If you are indeed Rupert's son," exclaimed John Langley, defending himself without attacking in return, "you are a rebel and an outlaw, whom all good subjects are bound to capture or punish."

"I am neither," said Rupert, dropping the point of his rapier; "I have this day received the King's permission to enter his service, through the intercession of Sir Stephen Compton, who sent his servants to assist me in rescuing the Baroness Langdale—my lady—my wife—from you. Look at their liveries and satisfy yourself. Your game is over, crafty bloodhound! your schemes defeated; yet will you not receive the full measure due to your iniquities! Conduct Lady Langdale downstairs, D'Arcy. The first who stirs to follow is a dead man." Rupert drew a pistol from his belt, cocked and presented it.

"My barkers are below," cried Harold, who had attempted to interpose two or three times, but had been disregarded—"My barkers are below, or you should not have it all your own way."

"Be silent," said his father, turning on him, his cheek ashy pale, the blood sprung on his lip where he had pressed his teeth, in the rage of baffled craft—"there is no more to be said now." He sheathed his sword with a sudden click, and stood looking silently on the floor, already, no doubt, planning how he should colour the affair in explaining it to his chief.

Meanwhile, Rupert backed slowly from the room, keeping his eyes fixed on the men opposed to him, then darted quickly downstairs. At the foot he found Sir Stephen Compton's two servants waiting sword in hand to defend the retreat of D'Arcy and Maud, who stood in the doorway, the light, which was still strong in the west, falling on their figures. Maud was clasping his arm with both her hands, her face turned to his shoulder as if to shut out the place from her sight.

Rupert sprang to her side, as soon as he had uncocked his pistol and thrust it in his belt.

"Lean on me, dear cousin. Quick, D'Arcy —the horses! Come, my good Hammond, let us to your master's as fast as we can."

They hurried to the front of the house where the horses had been tied to the palings and a stunted, broken tree.

"How shall we convey you?" cried Rupert to Maud. "You tremble as if you could scarce stand; suffer me to hold you!" He passed his arm round her with a tender reluctance, dreading she might think he would presume upon the admission she had just made. " Nor could you, I fear, keep your seat on horseback."

" Oh, do not trouble about my strength ! I am well able to walk—only take me away to a place of safety, dear Rupert ! I cannot ·breathe here !" and too terrified and distraught by the violent scene she had just witnessed, and the long strain her nerves had endured, to think of delicate scruples, she clung closely to him, while he felt her heart throb wildly under his supporting hand.

" Be comforted, dear heart," he whispered lovingly. " You are safe ; all will be well. I am taking you to a good kind lady who will cherish you !" Then, turning to the rest : " Keep close round us," he said ; " though I do not fear the slightest molestation. John Langley will never resist law or authority. Yet, let us put some distance between us and that accursed house !"

" Ah, Dorothy ! where is Dorothy ?" murmured Maud, suddenly stopping.

"She is also safe and well. She is following in our footsteps, and will soon be here.
Then you will have her companionship on the
way to Sir Stephen Compton's."

"I shall have Dorothy! Oh, thank God,
all will indeed be well! See! I am better
and stronger already. I can walk now with
the help of your arm, kindest cousin."

She drew herself gently from him, but
held his arm with both hands, looking up in
his face trustingly, with grateful tear-gemmed
eyes; so that Rupert, though anxious to see
her safe, was for a moment wrapped in a haze
of heavenly happiness, and ever since declared
that his idea of paradise was inseparably asso-
ciated with a background of wide, scrubby,
desolate common.

"She ought to be here by this time, though
a coach travels but slowly! Your man, is he
prompt and intelligent?" said Rupert to
Hammond.

"He is, sir; he will execute orders punc-
tually and satisfactorily."

A few more paces in silence. and then
D'Arcy said :

" I hear horses and wheels ; I will ride on and hasten them."

They had by this time neared a second clump of trees—solemn, ghostly poplars—and round it came, to Maud's joy, a coach, accompanied by a man on horseback ; while from the window protruded a head, and hand at arm's length, both shaking and gesticulating vehemently.

The next moment that excellent creature, Dorothy, had darted out with a bound, and had caught her darling lady in her arms.

" Oh, my jewel! my honey! are you safe and well ? Oh, sir! Master Monteiro, I hope you and D'Arcy have not left a whole bone in one of them villains' skins ! My darling! you are all of a thrimble, and no wonder ! Ah, speak to me !"

But Maud could only kiss and embrace her faithful nurse. She felt and seemed exhausted. She was glad to enter the carriage, and leaning against Dorothy, who supported her in her arms, to counteract the rough jolting which they endured.

Rupert rode by the carriage door, and from

his intermittent talk with Dorothy, Maud had gathered particulars of her aunt's base treachery, which but for poor Letitia Sparrow, would have resulted in the ruin of her happiness for life. She shuddered to think how narrow had been her escape. Dorothy also detailed her own sufferings : how when, to her surprise, she found her door at length unlocked, she sallied downstairs, and met the master of the house, who expressed his great regret at the unfortunate accident ; the door had been locked by mistake, no one knowing she was there ; whereupon Dorothy gave him a piece of her mind, *i.e.*, a torrent of vehement abuse, and, calling a chair, proceeded as fast as she could to Lady Helmsford's, where she found poor little Gomez, who had run away from Mistress Ferrars ; both were denied admittance, and then Dorothy came to the conclusion that Maud had been betrayed into John Langley's custody ; to his house Gomez was able to lead her, and while she was creating the disturbance we have described, the little negro slipped away to seek his all-powerful patron, Don Monteiro.

At last a smoother road and increasing houses showed they were once more within a civilised district ; and in another quarter of an hour they stopped before the great gates of Sir Stephen Compton's residence.

The door was quickly thrown open at the sound of their arrival, and as the light from the hall streamed out upon the dusk evening, Maud could see an elegant-looking gentleman and a tall lady advancing to the threshold.

Rupert assisted Maud to alight, and, closely followed by Dorothy, led her to her host.

"I have the honour of committing the Baroness Langdale to your care, Sir Stephen, in accordance with the Lord Chancellor, her legal guardian's direction," he said.

"It is with joy and pride I receive her," said the polite Baronet, kissing her hand, and then placing it in that of his daughter. "Mistress Compton will be charmed to receive you as a sister."

In effect, that kind lady embraced Maud with tears in her eyes, and conducted her into

the library, where supper was laid ; while Sir
Stephen gave orders that D'Arcy and the
rest should be hospitably entertained.

" What a day's work !" he exclaimed, as
Rupert gave a hasty sketch of the rescue.
" What a scoundrel that Langley is. Well,
at any rate, your fortune is made, my friend !
The young heiress will never part with so
gallant a husband."

" I do not think of that at present," returned Rupert, the thermometer of whose
hopes and joy had been steadily falling since
Maud had passed from his care. " She has
been sorely tried ; let her have time to
recover."

They entered the library, and found Maud,
Mistress Compton, and Dorothy standing
together, the two latter in eager conversation.

" We only waited your coming, sir," said
Mistress Compton. " Lady Langdale wishes
to say ' good-night ' and a few words to her
brave preserver !"

" To whom I owe everything," said Maud,
stepping forward—her pretty hat thrown off,

her bright brown hair in rich confusion. " Rupert "—she paused and looked down, the delicate colour mantling on her cheek—" I want to thank you—and I cannot."

She held out both her hands. Rupert sprang forward, clasped and kissed them.

" I want no thanks," he said in a low voice ; " I deserve none. Who would not strive to save that which is dearer than life ? but I shall see you to-morrow, when you will be calm, and not urged by feeling to admit more than your sober judgment would approve. Remember "—he looked round as he spoke, and again kissing Maud's hands, let them go gently—" remember, this dear lady is free of all claims from me ! whatever the urgency of her great danger may have induced her to admit ! Good-night, sweet cousin ! Sir Stephen, I have some way farther to ride. I must———"

He hesitated and half turned away ; his voice was unsteady, and had a degree of pathos in its tone which moved Maud strangely. She made a quick movement to him, and

clasped both her arms round his, pressing it
to her, and looking into his face, too earnest
in her desire to show her trust in his truth
and honour to shrink from his gaze.

"Ah, do not go! I only feel safe when
you are with me! Stay with me, dear
Rupert! stay with your wife!"

As she uttered the word deliberately, with
a slight pause before speaking it, she hid her
face against his shoulder with an inexpressibly
graceful gesture of abandonment to her love
for him, which sent all Rupert's brave resolu-
tions to be generous and self-denying to the
winds.

"My own—at last—my own!" he exclaimed, clasping his arms round her with
passionate delight, and, regardless of the onlookers, pressing his lips to hers in a long,
intense kiss—a kiss that to Maud was a
revelation.

"My dear sir," cried Sir Stephen, "this is
as it should be! The fair lady is quite right
—I trust you will not leave us to-night!
we counted on your company! and to-morrow
we will summon the worthy vicar of this

parish, and tie the nuptial-knot in a more orthodox fashion than it was originally! I give this advice seriously. We know not what may occur; but a real marriage, under the approval of His Majesty, cannot be interfered with! After the ceremony, you may go to my country-seat in Hertfordshire ('tis but a few hours' journey) for a short honeymoon; and I will to the King with a history of the romantic rescue and wedding. Shall it not be so, sweet Lady Langdale ?"

"It shall be as you all, good, kind friends, advise," said Maud softly, now palpitating and a little frightened at her own daring, though her hand still lay in Rupert's.

"And, at any rate," he remarked, "whatever fate may await the Heritage of Langdale, Maud Langley, my queen, my beloved, will be mine!"

Does the reader care to know more? We will hope so. All was done as sketched by the polite Sir Stephen.

The Government had no stancher adherent

than Sir Rupert Langley—as he became a year or two after—and early in George the Second's reign he was created Baron Langdale, in return for his diplomatic services.

John Langley, though defeated in his favourite scheme, was always a prosperous, though a gloomy man.

Harold, after a melancholy career as a "pretty fellow," "a beau," "a macaroni," was killed in a duel, arising out of a dispute at cards; after which his father seemed to lose all taste for public life, and became a mere miser. Dying intestate and without heirs, his property lapsed to the Crown.

Lady Helmsford long flourished—particularly in Paris—renowned for her bitter wit, and the brilliant society she gathered round her.

Her conversion to Romanism was one of the proudest achievements of M. l'Abbé de Trébise (a fashionable directeur). She lived to what is usually termed a "good old age."

Langdale Priory was a happy home—love

and truth flourished there—and the sweet mistress was mistress indeed : yet did she not fail to share her husband's wider and larger aims and interests. Ever returning from the gay world, where she was sought and respected, with deepest delight to the nest where her young birds grew in health and beauty.

The villagers, thriving in the neighbourhood of a resident landlord who cared for their prosperity, delighted to meet the little lord and ladies, in charge of a solemn, gaunt, grim old man with grey moustache—worn foreign fashion—who was their tutor in all manual exercises and horsemanship, while the authoritative Mistress Dorothy ruled the women, and even dominated the men, save one — a black page or footman of my lady's — who generally kept the servants' hall in a roar by his humorous absurdities.

Old Merrick still presided at the Crown and Sceptre. His favourite tale, when well warmed with prime October, was the strange adventures of the day when Captain Langley's horse broke loose, and he himself was kidnapped, with all the wondrous results which sprang from the weird wedding of the Heiress of Langdale.

THE END.

BILLING AND SONS, PRINTERS, GUILDFORD, SURREY.

www.ingramcontent.com/pod-product-compliance
Lightning Source LLC
Chambersburg PA
CBHW030634030726
47497CB00006B/1777